OUT OF THE DARKNESS

Between the ridge top and the camp, the ground was fairly clear of brush. Dusk had come, and down below him Jim could see the dark bulk of camp and corral. Waco had the door open, and the firelight cast a welcome glow. Lifting his voice, Jim called: "Hiyah . . . Waco!"

There was no answer. Briefly the spot of light was blotted out, and then showed again as someone crossed the door.

Jim stopped Monte beside the corral, swung down, and reached up for the saddle strings that held the sack. As he raised the knot, Monte, frightened, shied suddenly, and as he moved, a blow from the darkness grazed Jim's hat, knocking it off, and striking against his shoulder.

Momentarily confused by the swiftness of the unexpected attack, Jim went down, rolling on his side, his shoulder numb. As he rolled, he heard Waco's voice, a high squall: "Look out, Jim! They're . . ."

The voice broke off. Above Jim Barre flame ringed the muzzle of a gun, gravel spurted into his face, stinging against his cheek, and a shot crashed, almost deafening him with its nearness. . . .

THE
MEXICAN
SADDLE

BENNETT FOSTER

LEISURE BOOKS   NEW YORK CITY

A LEISURE BOOK®

June 2003

Published by special arrangement with Golden West Literary Agency.

Dorchester Publishing Co., Inc.
276 Fifth Avenue
New York, NY 10001

ISBN: 0-8439-5199-0

The name "Leisure Books" and the stylized "L" with design are trademarks of Dorchester Publishing Co., Inc.

Printed in the United States of America.

Visit us on the web at www.dorchesterpub.com.

THE
MEXICAN
SADDLE

One

Death Comes Double

A morning-after inspection of Carver City brought to light certain facts that excitement and dusk had concealed. In front of the hotel Mr. James Barre and Mr. Waco Gus Ibolt, recently of the K Cross cow outfit, savored the dark brown taste of their mouths and surveyed the little town with jaundiced eyes. Down in the stockyards some five hundred head of K Cross calves lifted mournful voices, lamenting the mothers that were far away, and in front of the Home Ranch Saloon a solitary swamper languidly swept the sidewalk. Removing their gaze from this depressing scene, Jim Barre and Waco stared at each other.

"It looked a lot better last night," Mr. Barre asserted.

"A heap better." Waco paused for thought, and then pursued the subject. "When I first come out, I thought it looked this way because I was empty. I done et, an' it looks just the same."

There was little further to say concerning Carver City, and Jim Barre said it. "Mebbe," he suggested tentatively, "we'd ought to hit for El Paso."

Waco looked glum. "After last night," he pointed out, "I wouldn't last no four months in El Paso. She'd be too swift for me. What I need is a job."

There was a pause during which both men considered the previous evening, its delights, entertainment, and expense.

"There ain't no chance of ketchin' on with the K Cross again," Waco observed moodily. "They done hired their winter hands."

"I got a hundred dollars," Jim said, brightening. "We ain't broke yet, Waco."

"But we're goin' to be." Waco could not see the sunny side of the affair. "We got horses an' saddles that we could hock, an' we got our beds, but how long would that last?"

"Not long, if we go like we did last night," Jim agreed. "But we could pinch her down some."

Waco snorted. "All summer an' fall," he said, "we been figgerin' on hivin' up this winter an' takin' things easy. We come to town an' blow our rolls in one night. An' both of us was so proud an' uppity that we turned down winter jobs. With just your hundred dollars, by spring we'd be ridin' grub line. What we got to do is go to work, an' you know it."

The prospect of labor, coupled with a first-class headache, furrowed Jim Barre's forehead. But what Waco had said was true.

"I'm goin' back upstairs an' think about it," the older man announced. "I got up at four o'clock after I'd promised myse'f I'd sleep. I'm so danged used to hearin' Coosie holler . . . 'Roll out!' . . . that, when four o'clock comes, I wake up standin' beside my bed an' reachin' for my pants. You comin'?"

Jim shook his head. "I'm goin' down an' watch the boys load calves," he answered. "I'm goin' to sit on the top rail of the pen an' give 'em good advice an' watch 'em sweat in the dirt."

"An' get yourse'f shot, too," Waco prophesied darkly. "Go on, then. I'm goin' to get my sleep out." He turned and, carrying his five feet and five inches of height with dignity, moved toward the hotel entrance. Jim Barre walked slowly down the street.

At the corner, Jim paused. The stockyards were two blocks away, and, in the bright November sun, dust was already lifting from the pens. The K Cross was loading calves. Had they so desired, both Waco Ibolt and Jim Barre could now be engaged in that activity. They had both been offered winter jobs at the K Cross, but they had refused. To Jim's immediate left was a saddle shop. Jim turned to the window and idly peered through the glass. There was a saddle set up on a wooden horse.

The saddle was old. Brush-scarred *tapaderos* covered the stirrups, and the skirts were deep and heavy. Someone had left a set of spur tracks across the seat, and the rawhide-covered horn, big as a pie plate, was deeply marked where many a dally had been snugged. The saddle was a three-quarter rig without a flank cinch, and there was no question as to its origin. It had come from Mexico. On the corners of the skirts the marks still showed where silver ornaments had been removed. Intrigued, Jim stood looking through the window and speculated concerning the saddle and its history. A card gave the price: **$10.00.**

"Jim!"

The word and quick steps on the board sidewalk caused Jim Barre to turn. "Hello, Dale," he greeted.

Dale Clark, young, black-haired, and brown-eyed, smiled uncertainly. He, too, had once been a part of the K Cross crew. Now, like Barre, he was unemployed for the winter. "I just came from the hotel," he announced. "Waco said you were goin' down to the stockyards."

"Headed that way," Jim agreed. "I thought I'd go down an' encourage the boys a little while they loaded. You comin'?"

Clark shook his head. "Not now," he said. "Jim . . . ?" It was plain that he was embarrassed.

"What you got on your mind, Dale?"

Clark hesitated and then blurted out his errand. "Could

9

you loan me some money, Jim?"

Jim touched the thin roll of bills in his pocket. Dale Clark was a K Cross boy. All summer long and all fall Jim Barre and Dale Clark had ridden for the same outfit, slept side by side, eaten together, but other than that Barre knew nothing about Clark. The boy was close-mouthed, watchful, and self-sufficient, and a good hand.

"How much do you need?" Jim asked.

Clark's brown eyes lighted. "All I can get," he said eagerly. "I can pay it back tomorrow. I wouldn't ask you, but I've got to have it."

There was something about the eagerness, some queer restraint on the part of the younger man, that aroused Jim's curiosity. "You in trouble, Dale?" he asked.

"No!" Clark sounded positive. "No trouble."

Jim extended the money. "There's a hundred dollars," he drawled. "It's all I've got, Dale. Will that do you?"

Clark took the bills eagerly. "It's enough," he said. "I'll bring this back tomorrow, Jim. Down to the hotel."

Barre nodded. He could still sense the restraint, the eagerness, and the tension of the other, and it prompted him to say: "If you're in trouble, you can always get help, Dale."

"Thanks." Clark started toward the door of the saddle shop, paused, and turned back. "You were goin' to the stockyards," he said, as though reminding Barre of his destination.

"An' if I don't get down there, I can't help the boys load," Jim grinned. "So long, Dale." He nodded and moved on, rounding the corner and walking toward the dust-clouded pens at the end of the street. He had gone perhaps ten feet when he heard the screen door of the saddle shop bang shut. It sounded as though Dale Clark had entered the building.

At noon, returning the way he had come, Jim Barre passed

10

the saddle shop. Idly he noted that the saddle was gone from the window. A display of bridles, spurs, and spur leathers had supplanted it.

In their room Jim found Waco Ibolt stretched out on the bed, boots removed, and a cigarette projecting from his graying mustache.

"I see," Waco commented without turning his head, "that you got back without bein' killed. Either the boys took pity on your ignorance or you kept your mouth shut."

Jim disregarded the statement. "It's time to eat," he announced.

Waco made no move to rise. "I been thinkin'," he declared, "an' I got our winter figgered out."

"Yeah?"

"Yeah. We're goin' wolf trappin'."

En route to the washstand, Jim stopped. "Wolf trappin'?"

"Yeah," Waco replied placidly. "We'll take that hundred dollars you got an' buy some traps an' some grub. We'll need pack mules, too. Then we'll go trap wolves. The state is payin' a ten-dollar bounty on 'em, an' five for coyotes. We can get twenty for a mountain lion."

"An' where are we goin' to trap all these wolves?"

"Down to the Chisos." Waco was still calmly dogmatic. "There's more wolves down there than" — he paused for a moment to think of a metaphor — "than there is cowpunchers in hell!"

"That's a lot of wolves." Jim resumed his progress to the washstand. "We go down to the Chisos an' starve on your cookin', an' freeze, an' trap? That's the devil of an idea." Secretly Jim thought it a very good idea, indeed, but, given his natural contrariness, he could not immediately agree with Waco. But he was looking at Waco as he moved and, as a result, stumbled over something at the foot of the bed. Investi-

11

gating the obstacle, he noted for the first time the old saddle, lying on its side.

"Where'd that come from?" Jim demanded, kicking the saddle.

"Dale Clark brought it up here," explained Waco. "Said he wanted you to keep it for him. Said that it was security."

Jim Barre exploded. "Security . . . be damned! I loaned him a hundred dollars, an' he brings me that saddle for security. I saw it in a window this mornin', an' the price was ten dollars."

Waco sat up on the bed. "You loaned Clark a hundred bucks?" he demanded, staring incredulously at his friend.

"He needed it for somethin', an' he said he'd bring it back tomorrow," Jim said defensively.

Waco laughed. "So he brung this old saddle up here," he jibed, "an' left it to secure his loan."

"Dale Clark's good for a hundred," Jim announced sturdily. "We punched cows with that boy since last April an' . . ."

"An' you don't know a damned thing about him," Waco completed. "Mebbe he's good for it, an' mebbe he ain't. You'll never know until tomorrow." Having delivered this pronouncement, he pulled on a boot. "An'," he concluded, "if Clark don't pay you back, you always got this saddle."

"Put on that other boot an' let's go eat," Jim ordered. "Dale will pay me. An' I don't want to hear any more about it."

His voice was clipped, final. He himself was beginning to doubt his wisdom in loaning Dale Clark his entire bank roll. Waco opened his mouth to speak further and then, after a glance at his friend, thought better of the idea. Jim Barre and Waco Ibolt had been together a long time. They were friends and had been side by side through some pretty rough places. When Jim used just that tone of voice, Waco kept silent.

"An' we can talk about your fool wolf-trappin' idea while we eat," Jim said. "I ain't sayin' that I'll go on it, but it won't hurt to listen."

Waco grunted as the other boot went on. He and Jim Barre would be trapping that winter. There would be a lot of argument and wrangling, but Waco knew they would trap just the same.

Dinner finished, the two wandered out of the hotel dining room and onto the street. There Waco challenged Jim to a game of rotation pool and was promptly accepted. Like many another cowhand, the two fancied themselves as pool players. They went to the Elite pool hall, and, when Jim won the first game, Waco was not content.

The dispute over their respective skills waxed hot between them, and could only be satisfied by more pool. As a result, it was nearing five o'clock when they were interrupted in their pastime. Bill Murry, constable of Carver City, and Stupe Wadell, his night deputy, came into the pool hall and, after speaking to the proprietor, came on back to the table, where the two 'punchers were playing.

Before becoming night marshal of Carver City, Stupe Wadell had punched cows and served a part of an enlistment with the rangers, and the blank-faced, rawboned officer was well-known throughout the country. Rumor had it that he had been discharged from ranger service because of certain irregularities, but no one ever questioned the man about the reason for his discharge. Wadell's temper was uncertain. He was handy with a gun and not above taking advantage of any official position he might occupy.

Murry, on the other hand, was a short, roly-poly, middle-aged man everybody liked. He used tact rather than force in handling his office, but no one had ever accused him of lacking courage. The two, Stupe Wadell and Bill Murry, made an efficient team, and Carver City was more or less proud of its law officers.

"What have you men got on your minds?" Jim Barre asked after the greetings had been exchanged. "You look solemn as a tree full of owls."

Murry nodded his head toward the door. "Wish you'd come with us," he said. "Got somethin' to show you. We been lookin' for some K Cross hands."

"We ain't with the K Cross no more," Waco announced, "but I reckon we'll do. It's a good thing you come in when you did. I was cleanin' Jim's plow."

"You an' who else?" Jim retorted. "Sure, we'll come with you, Bill. What's wrong?"

"I'll show you," Murry answered. "Come on." He stepped aside, allowing Waco and Jim Barre to precede him.

Outside the Elite the officers fell in beside each other, and Waco and Jim, following them, exchanged questioning glances. Bill Murry had not been his usual smiling self. His face was grave and worried. Wadell's countenance was blankly inscrutable.

"This is pretty bad, boys," Murry said over his shoulder. "You ain't goin' to like it. But me an' Stupe had to have some help, an' we figgered you could give it to us."

"What is it, Bill?" Jim asked again.

"You'll see in a minute," Murry answered.

They were at a corner now, and the officers turned left, leading the way toward the section of Carver City known as Chihuahua. Here, in small adobes, the native population of the town made their homes. The men passed by houses whose occupants stared at them curiously, past a few loiterers, and then, reaching the outskirts of the section, came to a small, square adobe set well apart from all neighboring

14

buildings. Murry paused, looked at Jim and Waco, and then pushed open the door.

"Inside," he said tersely.

Entering the room, Jim paused for an instant to let his eyes adjust themselves to the dim light. Waco pushed past, and Murry entered behind him. Stupe Wadell remained at the door, leaning against the door jamb.

Growing accustomed to the gloom of the room, Jim could see a huddle of clothing in one corner. A boot projected from the clothing, and, stepping closer, he saw another boot beside the first. A pallid, blood-smeared face stared up at him from a single eye. The other eye had been gouged out, the eye socket gaping red and ghastly. Jim caught his breath sharply.

"Dale Clark," he gasped.

"My gentle Nelly!" Waco rasped, using the pet oath he reserved for special occasions.

"Who killed him?" Jim, partially recovered from his first shock, glared at Murry.

The marshal shook his head. "That's what we want to know," he drawled. "That's why we brought you here."

"You don't think that Jim or me . . . ?" Waco began harshly.

Murry's drawling voice checked the words. "No. We know where you boys were. But we thought that mebbe you'd know somebody that had it in for Clark."

Waco and Jim stared at each other. Waco shook his head. Jim, turning, spoke again to Murry. "No. We don't. . . ."

At the doorway, Stupe Wadell's bass voice growled a command. "Hold it! Stop! Stop, you!"

The other men in the little room looked in that direction.

Wadell moved away from the door, and they could see only one booted foot of his and part of a leg. "Stop, damn

15

you!" Wadell called, and, following swiftly upon the words, a gun roared.

Bill Murry, pulling a pistol from his holster, leaped to the door. Jim took a step to follow, and was stopped by Waco's hand on his arm. Neither man was armed. It was against the law to carry guns in town. "Easy!" Waco commanded.

Murry was out of the door now, and gone. Wadell's leg had disappeared. Barre, throwing off Waco's restraint, made for the opening, and his friend followed. They stepped out into the dimming afternoon light. There, perhaps twenty feet away, Wadell stood, legs spread, arm lifted. Murry was running toward Wadell, and beyond the deputy marshal, perhaps fifty feet away, a man crawled along the ground, trying desperately to reach the shelter of a pile of posts. Even as the two watched, Wadell's arm bounced and his gun roared once more. The crawling man jerked, came halfway up, and then fell twitching, not four feet from the post pile. As one, the four men ran forward.

The fallen man had rolled to his back when the second shot finished him, and he lay now, sprawled out, his mouth agape, and sightless eyes staring at the sky. Beyond one outflung arm, just at the tips of the fingers, was the black butt of a gun. Bill Murry, looking down, said: "Pancho Vigil. Stupe, you. . . ."

"He came out from behind the 'dobe," interrupted Wadell. "He wouldn't stop, when I yelled at him. I seen his gun."

Murry said — "Hmm." — very thoughtfully.

Bending down, Waco Ibolt touched the silver buckle of the dead man's belt, straightened, and turned to look at the marshal.

"That's Dale Clark's belt," he said harshly. "Stupe didn't make no mistake."

Murry turned to Jim Barre for confirmation and received it. Jim had seen that silver-mounted belt too many times to be mistaken. Wadell grunted with gratification.

"That settles it, then," he said heavily. "It was Pancho that killed Clark. Pancho always was a bad Mexican."

Murry searched his big deputy with his eyes, and then looked at Jim Barre. "You boys will have to be witnesses at the inquests," he said quietly. "I'll tell you when. Let's get Pancho into the shack an' send uptown for a wagon. Come on, Stupe. Help me lift him."

"We'll get the wagon," Waco offered.

Murry nodded. He bent then, grunting as his paunch offered objection to the movement.

"Come on, Stupe," he said again. "You take his feet."

Waco touched Jim Barre's arm. "Let's go," he said.

Walking away from the outlying adobe, Jim looked back. Murry and Wadell were carrying Pancho's limp body through the door.

Waco also had looked back. Now, turning his head again, he made a gruff comment. "The danged fool hung around. Just like a Mexican!"

For perhaps a hundred yards the two walked in silence. They were entering the more densely populated portion of the Mexican section now, and again dark faces stared at them from behind windows. Chihuahua, used to violence, wanted no part of this.

"Wadell," Waco said suddenly, "is mighty handy with a gun. Mighty handy. It looks to me like, after he dropped Pancho, he could've disarmed him. That Mexican was hurt the first shot. You seen him crawlin'."

"He was headed for the post pile." Jim's voice was reflective. "If he'd got behind it, he might've been tough to take."

"That's so," Waco agreed. Then: "Did you see the way

17

Clark was cut up? Had an eye gouged out."

Involuntarily Jim Barre shuddered. "He must have put up a scrap," he said.

"No!" Waco shook his head. "There wasn't no sign of it, an', anyhow, Clark's hands were tied."

"Tied?"

"Sure. Tied behind him."

Again there was a silence. Then Jim said: "What was the idea of that, I wonder?"

Two

The Inquest

The inquests were held at ten o'clock. Until the early-morning hours, Waco Ibolt and Jim Barre had been besieged by questions. They had told the story of the two deaths perhaps twenty times, always to a curious audience, and, had they taken all the drinks offered them in the Home Ranch and the Blue Ribbon, they might have gotten drunk as many times as they had told the tale. Now, as they walked toward the Pastime Dance Hall, where the inquests were to be held, each was wondering if he could tell the same tale again. So many questions had been asked and answered, so many conjectures advanced, so much rumor had been retailed to them, that they were doubtful of what they really did know.

"We just tell what we seen," Waco observed, stopping in front of the Pastime. "That's all, ain't it?"

"Just what we saw, an' nothin' else," agreed Jim.

Entering the Pastime, they found a crowd already assembled to hear the details of the inquest. Ensconced behind a table close beside the stove was the justice of the peace, and grouped to the left of the justice was a jury of six men, looking uneasy and out of place. Stupe Wadell and Bill Murry were seated close to the table, and, on improvised tables of trestles and boards from which the Ladies' Aid occasionally served a dance crowd, there were two, long, shrouded shapes. Seated near the stove, her back half turned to the crowd, was a dark-haired girl, neatly dressed, a suitcase on the floor beside her chair.

Murry nodded somber greeting as Waco and Jim came up

and, lowering his voice to a whisper, said: "Just about ready."

"Old Griggs always fools around," Wadell growled. "He's so blasted important, you'd think he was the corpse."

Griggs, the justice of the peace, glared at the night marshal and resumed his conference with the jury foreman, who leaned on the table.

Murry nodded his head toward the girl who sat beside the stove. "Clark's sister," he whispered. "She come in on the train this mornin'."

Waco and Jim stared at the girl.

Griggs cleared his throat. "We'll proceed, gentlemen," he announced importantly. The foreman of the jury returned to the group and sat down beside his fellows.

A doctor was first called to testify. He swore to the fact that he had been called to examine the body of Dale Clark and ascertain the cause of death, and that Dale Clark had died from wounds inflicted by a knife. The doctor, excused, sat down, and Bill Murry was called.

Murry told how he had been summoned to Chihuahua by a Mexican woman who, returning from her daily work, had found a dead man in her house. The officer continued, telling of how he had called his night deputy and how, together, they had gone to the house, found the body, and what steps they had taken in the matter. When Murry finished his testimony, María Sandoval, who had first found the body, was called.

María, through a court-appointed interpreter, disclaimed any knowledge of what had happened in her house. She had been, she said, washing clothes for Mrs. Griggs that day — a fact which the justice confirmed with a nod. The woman was dismissed, and Stupe Wadell was called. He explained how his presence had been brought about and told of the occurrences at the adobe, climaxing his testimony by a briefly recounted statement concerning the killing of Pancho Vigil.

Waco and Jim Barre, in turn, were called to the stand and told what they knew, each identifying Dale Clark's silver-mounted belt, when it was presented for inspection, and testifying that they had seen the belt about the body of Pancho Vigil. Following their testimony, there was a brief pause, and then Griggs, clearing his throat again, said: "Miss Clark, do you feel like testifying?"

Beside the stove, the girl, who had been crying quietly, raised a tear-stained face and nodded.

"What's he want to question her about?" Jim whispered fiercely to Waco. "She's feelin' plenty bad right now."

"I'll tell anything I know," the girl said, and moved toward the witness chair.

Jim, Waco, the whole room, watched her as she walked. There was a grace about the girl, a lithe sureness of movement. Her face, flushed as it was with weeping, was proud, and she held herself erect.

"Anybody'd know she was Dale's sister," Waco whispered. "Looks like him, only better."

The girl sat down. Answering Griggs's first question, she said she was Marilee Clark, and resided near Saunders.

"Dale Clark was your brother?" Griggs asked.

"My twin brother."

The justice of the peace harrumped deep in his throat. "Now, Miss Clark," he said, "when did you last hear from your brother?"

"Yesterday." The answer came clearly. "I had a telegram from him. He wanted me to meet him here today and bring what money I could. I took the train last night."

"And had your brother any enemies that you know of?"

The girl considered the question. "He had enemies," she said slowly. "But I don't think. . . ." She stopped, averting her face from the curious eyes that stared at her, and was plainly

21

fighting for self-control.

"We know who killed Dale," Jim Barre whispered to Murry. "Stop that old fool, Bill. That girl's had all she can stand."

Murry, moving swiftly to the desk, bent down and whispered to Griggs. The justice listened, and then nodded.

"That will do, Miss Clark," he announced. "You may step down. Does the jury have any questions to ask this witness?"

The jury, plainly suffering with the girl, had none. Marilee Clark, rising from the witness chair, found Bill Murry beside her. The marshal led her back to her seat beside the stove.

"The jury will consider their verdict," Griggs directed.

The jurymen whispered among themselves. In the crowd voices murmured, questions and answers tossing back and forth. Jim watched the girl beside the stove as she pressed her eyes with a wisp of handkerchief.

Returning to their table, Murry said: "It oughtn't to take long."

On the heels of that statement the jury foreman came to his feet and announced: "We reached a verdict."

"You will state it," Griggs directed.

"Dale Clark was killed by Pancho Vigil," the jury foreman stated. "The motive was robbery. An' Pancho was killed by an officer in the performance of his duty." He sat down.

Griggs scowled. "We haven't held the other inquest yet," he reproved. "You got to hear all the evidence before you can reach a verdict on Pancho."

"We done reached a verdict on Pancho," the foreman stated stubbornly. "The evidence is just the same. Pancho was wearin' Clark's belt . . . so he killed Clark . . . an' there ain't no question about who shot Pancho . . . an' damn' good riddance, too."

Having delivered this peroration, the foreman left his

chair, the remainder of the jury rising and flanking him.

"I got to get back to the store," the foreman announced. "An' the rest of these boys got to go to work. That's all, Judge."

"Here, wait a minute!" Griggs, his dignity offended, started up from behind his table. "You got to write these verdicts out an' sign 'em. You got. . . ."

"You bring 'em around to the store, Judge," the foreman drawled, starting toward the door. "I'll sign 'em there. Come on, boys."

The jury, donning their hats, followed the foreman. Murry was grinning widely, and Waco frankly giggled. Judge Griggs, his self-importance swept away, was frantically gathering papers together from the table top.

"Kind of sunk his bobber," Waco said. "He'd've kept them boys here all day. You want us for anything more, Bill?" he asked.

"I don't think so." Murry shook his head.

Marilee Clark, carrying her suitcase, was moving toward the door. Jim Barre, following the girl with his eyes, was roused from his thoughts by Waco's touch.

"We can go home now," Waco said gently.

Outside on the street, the crowd from the inquest pouring out behind them, Waco and Jim turned toward the hotel. Ahead of them Marilee Clark walked, still carrying her suitcase. Jim started forward, and Waco kept pace.

"Let me carry that, Miss Clark," Jim said awkwardly, when he reached the girl's side.

She looked at him, startled, as he sought to possess himself of the handle of her bag.

"I'm Jim Barre," he said. "This is Waco Ibolt. We punched cows with your brother on the K Cross. We're mighty sorry about what happened."

23

Without answering, the girl released the suitcase handle so that Jim could carry the grip.

"If there's anything we can do," Jim continued, ill at ease, "all you got to do is to tell us. We. . . ." He stopped. It was plain that Marilee Clark was not listening, that she was moving in a sort of trance. Looking across to Waco, Jim shook his head. This was bad, plenty bad.

Reaching the hotel, Waco held the door open, allowing the girl and Jim to enter. The two men accompanied her to the foot of the stairs, and there, stopping, Marilee Clark reached for the grip.

"You've been very kind," she said. "I know . . . Dale mentioned you when he wrote to me. I. . . ." She choked on a sob and started blindly up the stairs.

Jim and Waco watched her go. There was nothing that they could do, no help that they could offer, no consolation. The feeling of helplessness made them savage.

"Damn it!" Waco rasped. "I wish it had been me that downed that Mexican."

Jim, watching Marilee Clark disappear around the turn of the staircase, made no reply.

The two men turned away from the stairway and, finding chairs in the lobby, sat down. For a long while there was no talk between them. Not until Bill Murry came in and seated himself to Jim's right did either speak. Then, nodding to Bill, Waco voiced a comment.

"She's all alone," he said. "Hang it. Why does a thing like this have to happen to a girl like that? She ain't got nobody with her an'. . . ."

"My wife's comin'," Murry interrupted. "I'll take her up when she gets here."

Again the moody silence.

Jim Barre broke it next. "Anythin' we can do about makin'

24

arrangements an' such," he said, "you just speak up, Bill."

"I'll tend to that," Murry answered. "It's kind of my job. I wish my wife 'u'd get here."

As though in answer to the wish, Mrs. Murry, plump, motherly, and capable, came through the door. Murry stepped forward to meet her.

"The girl's upstairs, Jane," he announced. "I'll take you right up."

When the marshal and his wife were gone, the two men lingered in the hotel lobby. Above the clerk's desk the big clock ticked, and Waco, looking at it, made a statement.

"Half past twelve."

"I don't feel hungry," Jim said, interpreting Waco's words.

"Funny." Waco still looked at the clock. "I don't, neither. But I need a drink. You comin', Jim?"

"I'll stay here a while," Jim answered.

Waco hesitated, apparently undecided, then turned toward the door.

"I'll be back," he said briefly, and went on out.

Waco had not yet returned when Murry came back downstairs. The marshal had information for Jim and business to transact. Murry's wife, he said, had talked to the girl, and was staying with her. In the meantime, there was a telegram to send, and arrangements to make.

"She wants to ship her brother back to Saunders on tonight's train," Murry announced. "She's goin' to bury him there. An' I got to get a coffin an' a box to ship it in. She's goin' back with him. You want to come with me, Jim?"

Jim Barre got up. As they walked together toward the door, the marshal spoke again. "They got no folks. She an' her brother were recently orphaned. It's tough. An' I don't think they had much money."

A thought struck Jim. "Did you find any money on Pancho?" he asked.

Murry shook his head briskly. "Not a cent," he answered. "Funny, too. He robbed Clark of that belt an' that seemed to be all he got. Guess he hid the rest some place. We'll find it."

Jim Barre thought of his hundred dollars and shrugged. Now was not the time to advance a claim. And there never would be a time to advance a claim — not to that girl.

"I got to send a telegram to old Thad Gaskin," Murry said. "He's got a store down below Saunders, an' the girl works for him. Then we'll go pick out a box. Come on, Jim."

Side by side, the two swung off along the street toward the dépôt.

For the remainder of the day Jim Barre stayed with the marshal. From the dépôt they went to a store where, in a warehouse, they looked over coffins and selected one. Accompanying the boxed coffin back to the Pastime, they were met by Stupe Wadell.

Stupe, at Murry's direction, had turned Pancho Vigil's body over to some of his numerous relatives, who had taken it away. The big man helped unload the casket and aided in placing Dale Clark within it. When the men put on the lid, they screwed it down tightly.

"No use of her lookin' at that face," Murry said gruffly. "Lord, but he's cut up!"

"Tied his hands an' then carved on him," Jim said. "You did a good job when you shot Pancho, Stupe."

"Tied his hands?" Bill Murry stared at Jim. "His hands wasn't tied."

"Waco said they were," Jim answered. "I didn't see it myself."

Murry looked at his deputy. "Did you see that Clark's

hands were tied?" he demanded.

Wadell shook his head. "Waco was seein' things," he answered. "Clark's hands weren't tied."

Jim shrugged. "I guess Waco was mistaken," he said. "You boys ought to know. Come on, let's load this box an' get it to the dépôt."

The dray that had brought the coffin had waited, and the men carried their burden out of the Pastime and slid it into the bed of the dray. Wadell hopped up beside it to ride to the dépôt, and Murry and Jim Barre started back to the hotel. It was nearing train time.

In the lobby of the hotel Mrs. Murry was waiting with Marilee Clark. Her husband nodded to her, and the woman, slipping her arm beneath the girl's own, urged her toward the door.

Marilee allowed herself to be led away. Behind the two came Murry and Jim Barre, the latter carrying the girl's suitcase.

There was no talk at the dépôt. Bill Murry bought two tickets to Saunders, one for the girl, one for the body. They stood, silent, waiting for the train. A little knot of men, K Cross riders for the most part, formed on the dépôt platform, talking together in low voices.

The train came in, engine puffing, wheels clattering over the rail joints. Jim, standing beside the steps of the day coach, could see the express messengers and the dépôt agent loading the coffin into the express car. The conductor helped Marilee Clark up the step and swung her grip up to the car platform. Bending from the step, the girl kissed Mrs. Murry. Her voice was subdued when she spoke.

"Thank you all. You've been so kind."

" *'Boaaard!'* " the conductor called, and waved his paper-filled right hand.

The engine snorted. Bill Murry took his wife's arm, and Jim Barre, moving across the platform, joined the K Cross hands. They stood there, wordlessly, until the rear car was a dwindling dot along the rails.

"Guess that's it," said the K Cross man beside Jim. "We might as well go back uptown."

Once back in town Jim looked vainly for Waco. His partner had not been in the group on the platform of the station, and Jim strongly suspected that he would be found in one of the bars. Not that Waco was inclined to indulge, but occasionally he went on a bender, and, when he did, it was a good one.

The Home Ranch did not disclose Waco, nor did the Blue Ribbon. Two other saloons were equally barren. Leaving the last one, Jim encountered Stupe Wadell, and inquired of the deputy if he had seen Waco. Stupe had not seen Jim's partner, and the two men stood a moment together, Jim looking up and down the street as they talked.

"Waco's likely to be 'most any place," he said. "There's no tellin', if he's started on a drunk."

"Find him an' put him to bed," Wadell advised. "I don't like drunks runnin' loose when I'm on duty."

"I'll find him," promised Jim.

Wadell turned to walk away, and Bill Murry, coming along the street, stopped beside Jim. Wadell came back.

"You seen Waco?" Jim asked.

Murry shook his head. "No," he answered. "I haven't seen him. I'm goin' home to supper now, Stupe. I'll turn her over to you."

Wadell nodded and walked off again, and Jim, falling into step beside Murry, went back along the street.

"He's salty," Jim commented, jerking his head back toward Wadell's retreating figure. "And handy with a gun."

"Too handy!" Murry said sharply. "He didn't need to take that second shot at Pancho. We could've got him without killin' him."

"He'd have hung anyhow," Jim said.

"Yeah." Murry's answer was short. "But maybe there was somebody else in on that deal. If Pancho hadn't been killed, Pancho might've told us."

Barre stared curiously at the marshal. It was evident that all was not calm in the law-enforcement department of Carver City.

"Did Pancho have any friends?" Jim asked. "From what I heard at the inquest, he was kind of a tough *hombre* an' stayed by himself a lot."

"He did," Murry agreed. "But there's been a half-breed . . . Chink an' Mexican . . . around here, an' Pancho throwed in with him."

"What happened to the 'breed?"

Murry shrugged before he answered. "He's around. I ain't seen him for a day or so, but I'm goin' to look him up. Well, here's where I leave you. So long, Jim."

"So long."

The marshal turned and started down a side street, and Jim Barre, after a moment's hesitation on the corner, walked toward the hotel. It was the only place that he had not looked for Waco.

"Your partner's upstairs," the clerk said when Jim entered the lobby.

Waco sat tilted back in a chair in their room, his boots cocked up on the washstand and his hat resting beside him on the bed. The heavy odor of whiskey in the room, and the sparkle in Waco's eyes, testified that he had been indulging. It was also evident that Waco was pleased with himself. He waved a hand at Jim in a large and effulgent gesture.

"Come in an' set down. Have a drink," he invited. Concluding the wave, he pointed to the half-empty pint bottle on the dresser.

There was no use arguing with Waco, and no use in berating him. Jim intended to do neither. In his philosophy a man was entitled to get drunk if he wanted to. It was his headache. Jim came on into the room, picking up the pint as he passed the dresser, and, taking another chair, helped himself to a generous drink. He felt as though he needed one.

"I looked for you," Jim said. "If you wanted to go on a bender, why didn't you wait for me? I'd have gone with you."

"On my money?" Waco queried. "You went into the saddle business yesterday, remember? Now you're broke."

He held out his hand, and Jim passed the bottle.

"While you," Waco continued after he wet his whistle, "was indulging in weepin' an' tears an' gettin' stuck on that girl, I was tendin' to business. That's what I was doin'."

Jim looked at him expectantly. His partner was filled with a certain ebullience, an overflowing of spirit, as it were. Sober, Waco was a steady, dependable fellow that a man could count on, but, drunk, he broke out at unexpected places and odd angles.

"What have you been up to?" Jim demanded.

"I been financin' the wolf-trappin' business," Waco announced, and blinked owlishly at the lighted lamp. "An' I done it, too. I bought a mule an' a pack saddle, an' some groceries, an' some traps. An' I got a carton of Bull Durham an' some liquor." He thought a moment and then extended the bottle. "Most of the liquor's drunk," he said. "You better take another snort."

"Waco," Jim said sternly, accepting the bottle, "where'd you get the money? You didn't go borrowin', did you?"

Waco giggled foolishly and shook his head. "I didn't borrer," he answered. "I sold your saddle."

"You *what?*" Jim Barre sat down, holding the bottle in numbed fingers.

"Sold your saddle. For a hundred and fifty simoleons."

"A hundred and fifty dollars?"

"Yeah." Waco nodded to emphasize his words. "You had two, so I up an' sold the spare."

Jim Barre stared at his partner. Waco had done numerous things, but this transcended them all. This even beat the time in Fort Worth when, drunk as a fiddler at a dance, Waco had joined the fire department. That had taken considerable talk and ingenuity, but this had taken more. There was just one hundred and thirty-five pounds of Waco, but, when he untracked, he could cover more country and get into more difficulties than a man twice his size.

"I paid a hundred dollars for that saddle two years ago," Jim said sternly. "How did you sell it for a hundred an' fifty. You gypped somebody, Waco."

"I didn't, neither. I was in the Home Ranch takin' a drink an' wonderin' how we'd raise the money for an outfit. A feller come in an' stood next to me. Some way we got to talkin' about saddles, an' he said he wanted to buy one, so I sold him yours."

"He was drunk, an' so were you!" Jim accused.

"Mebbe." Waco was willing to admit the indictment. "But it wasn't up to me to look after him. Tradin' horses or sellin' saddles, a man's on his own judgment. That's the way I look at it. I tol' him that I had a nice saddle that I'd sell for a hun'erd an' fifty, an' we made the trade on the spot. You can ride that ol' saddle over there." He gestured to where the skirt of the old Mexican saddle protruded from beyond the end of the bed. A pregnant pause followed the movement.

In the silence following Waco's announcement, he hiccuped and hid his mouth politely with his hand. "We made the trade," he said, "an' I went down to the livery barn an' got your saddle an' borrered a sack an' fixed it all nice for him. When I brung it back, the feller paid me an' grabbed that saddle like it was a long-lost friend, an' lit a shuck for the dépôt. Last I seen of him, he was leggin' it that way. So then I went shoppin'."

Dimly Jim recalled having seen a sacked saddle on the truck that had hauled Clark's coffin to the express car. Even more dimly he recalled a man who had gotten into the smoker while the train was stopped. He shook his head.

"You beat me, Waco," he acknowledged.

"We had to do somethin'," Waco defended himself. "You'd blowed all your money goin' into the saddle business, so I had to he'p you out. Here's the balance of the money." He reached toward the bed, destroyed his perilous equilibrium, and struggled to regain it. In the struggle he knocked his hat to the floor, and there on the bed, where the hat had been, was a little pile of bills and silver. Regaining his balance, he smiled fondly at the money.

"It ain't enough to buy a good saddle for you," he announced, "but we can get mighty drunk on it. Let's do that. I already got a start. An' tomorrow we can pull out for the Chisos an' all them wolves that are a-waitin' for us."

Three

Gunpowder Greeting

"The Chisos," Waco drawled, "ain't much for mountains . . . if they was in Wyomin' or Colorado or New Mexico . . . but they're right good hills for Texas." He swayed in his saddle to dodge a projecting limb of mesquite, and Jim Barre, looking ahead toward the southeast, nodded his agreement.

This was the Big Bend country, rough, broken, and brushy, and there, not ten miles away, the Chisos were blue-black with growing dusk. The two men had been seven days coming from Carver City. One of those days had been spent at the K Cross, visiting, and that minor detour had added three days to the trip. In the main, Jim was enjoying himself, although Waco's undisturbed equanimity was a little hard to bear. A man just couldn't get a decent argument out of Waco.

The horses, keeping a steady walk, took either side of an ocotillo clump. The mule was following Waco. Jim's left *tapadero* scraped against the thorny growth, and he twisted in the seat of the Mexican saddle, so as to avoid more brush.

Jim liked the saddle. Old and worn slick with use, barren of any ornament or carving, still it was a mighty easy saddle to sit. The seat was comfortable, the cantle was neither too high nor too low, and the old A fork, terminating in the big, flat-topped horn, did not spread a man out. Jim Barre rode with a long stirrup, and so he really appreciated this saddle.

"Be there tonight," he announced. "Where'll we camp?"

"Plenty of places to camp," said Waco. "There's ol' cow-huntin' shacks all through the hills."

"An' what are the cowmen goin' to say about us squattin' down on their range?" Jim was still trying for an argument.

"Goin' to welcome us like prodigal sons," Waco assured him. "These fellers down here have been takin' as high as a ten-percent death loss from wolves. Damn it, Jim! We're apt to have to fight 'em off to keep 'em from kissin' us!"

"I ain't so sure of that," Jim objected. "Likely they'll think we're goin' to rustle somethin' of theirs an' take a shot at us."

"Naw!" Waco was scornful. "They all handle a few wet cows themselves, kind of on the side, an' the only folks they'll shoot at is Mexicans. I was down here with a V Cross T roundup one time. I know about this country."

"If you know about it, why did you ever come back?" Jim demanded as his horse slid down a little bank, reached the bottom, and began to climb. "Of all the rough, brushy, no-'count country in the world, this takes the prize! No grass, just a little water, an' more rocks than there is in a creek crossin'. Why a man that had got out of here would come back is past me."

"You" — Waco's voice conveyed his superiority — "don't like it 'cause you didn't pick it out. That's what's ailin' you. There's a cow camp up ahead, unless this trail I've hit is a liar. We'll lay over there tonight."

"An' I'll be glad to see somethin' besides mesquite, ocotillo, yucca, an' rocks," Jim growled. "Follow the trail, if you found one, an' don't talk so much about it."

Waco had, indeed, found a trail. His grulla horse — which for some unknown reason he insisted upon calling Oscar — swung into the faint path, and behind the grulla the pack mule dutifully followed. Jim reined in his own mount, a *bayo coyote,* after the mule, and the little caval-

34

cade went trotting along the trail.

"An' there's the camp," Waco announced triumphantly after perhaps fifteen minutes' riding. "Right where I said it would be."

The camp was a small rock building with one window and a door in the front wall. A dilapidated piece of stovepipe, serving for a chimney, projected through the dirt roof, and behind the house were a shed and a corral where four, saddled horses were tied. A loose horse in the corral lifted his head and nickered as Waco stopped, and, almost immediately following the sound, a tall man, tanned, wearing chaps, and with a sagging cartridge belt, appeared at the door. Jim stopped his buckskin beside Waco.

"Howdy," said the man in the doorway, his voice grating like the hinges of a disused gate.

"Howdy," Waco returned the greeting.

Proper etiquette indicated that the next words should come from the man in the door. This camp was his home — at least, he occupied it now — and, according to custom, he should have invited Jim and Waco to dismount. He did not. Instead, he stepped from the door, and the opening was immediately filled by another, so like the first in dress and appearance as to be his twin.

"We're travelin'," Waco announced. "Headin' for the Chisos. It's gettin' late." Here was a pointed hint.

Disregarding the not too subtle suggestion, the man who had first come out made a drawling comment. "Yo're on the right trail," he said. "Just keep on goin' southeast an' you'll hit 'em."

Waco glanced at his partner. A slow smile was beginning to form on Jim's face.

"We're wolfers," Waco said. "Goin' down there to trap."

"There's lots of wolves," agreed the tall man. "Good country to trap in."

Disgust and anger showed on Waco's face. Once more he glanced at Jim, who was now frankly smiling.

"You . . . ," Waco began, turning to the two at the house again.

What Waco had intended to say was lost. From inside the house a voice arose, high, shrill with agony.

"*¡Por diablos, señores!* I don' know. Lemme go. Please . . . lemme go!"

A curse and the thud of a blow preceded a scream. Waco, straightening, rapped out — "What you . . . ?" — and got no further. The man in the door dropped his hand out of sight behind the door jamb and brought it back, grasping a rifle, and the other man, outside the cabin, snatched a six-shooter from the holster at his hip, threw it up, and fired, all in one motion.

This was the Big Bend, where every man went armed. Waco Ibolt and Jim Barre might lay aside their weapons in Carver City, where the law demanded it, but they were not weaponless now. Even as his buckskin, grazed by the shot, whirled and almost unseated him, Jim Barre pulled his own gun. The snap shot he took was lucky and unlucky — lucky in that it chipped rock and dust from the wall beside the man in the doorway, thus blinding him for the moment, but unlucky in that it missed the rifleman.

Waco, squalling like an angry cat, was fighting the grulla and trying for a shot at the man with the short gun. The mule had stampeded back into the brush to the west, and there in the little clearing in front of the rock house pandemonium was loosed. Waco Ibolt and Jim Barre, not looking for trouble, but invited to it, were taking a helping.

For one instant Waco held the grulla down, and in that

fractional second he shot the man with the short gun, grazing his leg. The hawk-faced fellow buckled and went down, firing as he fell. Jim Barre, firing again despite the contortions of the buckskin that was earnestly trying to throw his rider and get away, sent a slug singing through the door, and the rifleman ducked back out of sight. As the buckskin came around again, pinwheeling and trying to get his head down to buck in earnest, Jim caught a glimpse of another face at the doorway. Then hot lead smacked the air beside him, and the doorway was filled with smoke and flame. Waco, purely mad and, as always, losing his head in a fight, tried vainly to force the grulla up to the house.

Jim regained control of his thoughts and the buckskin.

"Run, Waco!" he shouted. "Head that mule!"

Somehow the command carried through the little man's anger. He swung the grulla and made for the brush, and Jim, knowing that two mounted men could not hope to cope with riflemen on the ground, swung the buckskin and followed his partner. Together, not ten yards apart, they crashed into the screen of brush about the cabin and went smashing through, bent low in their saddles to avoid limbs and thorns that plucked at them.

Beyond the brush screen stretched a small open expanse, and at its farther side the mule was just disappearing. If they lost the mule, they lost their outfit, and Waco and Jim, without exchange of ideas, made for the mule.

The mule was not easy to catch. True, she carried a pack, but she was thoroughly alarmed, and she had the added advantage of the brush to screen her. A full fifteen minutes elapsed before Waco and Jim Barre cornered her. Then, with Waco holding the lead rope of the mule, the partners looked at each other.

It was almost dark. Jim's shirt had been ripped from

shoulder to belt by thorns, and Waco was not in much better condition. The little man's mustache bristled, and his face was contorted in a scowl.

"Them damned *ladrónes!*" he snarled. "I'm goin' back there an' . . . what you laughin' at?"

A grin had spread all across Jim Barre's square-cut, homely face. "At you," he retorted. "You was the one that said we'd have to fight these fellows off to keep 'em from kissin' us. We had to fight, all right, but not to keep from bein' kissed!"

Waco snorted indignantly. "You danged fool," he exploded. "They had somebody in that shack, workin' on him. I'm goin' back there!"

"An' get shot?" Jim said quietly, his face losing its smile. "Those boys are pretty sudden, Waco."

"Just the same, I'm goin' back," asserted his partner. "Nobody can cut down on me like that an' get away with it. I want to know who was in that shack. You comin'?"

"When it gets dark," Jim returned.

He was fully as angry as Waco, fully as determined. Whatever was taking place back there in the shack was bad. Safety dictated that Jim and Waco go on and put distance behind them. Curiosity and antagonism pushed safety aside. Jim Barre bent forward suddenly and spoke again.

"Listen!"

North of them there came the sound of movement in the brush.

Both men were bent forward intently, straining their ears. Jim's dun, Monte, cocked his ears and pointed his head toward the brush not a hundred yards away. Waco's grulla likewise looked toward the brush.

"Lookin' for us," Jim whispered.

As he spoke, he slid out a long arm and caught the cheek piece of the bridle, pulling Monte's head toward him. Waco duplicated the movement. Neither man wanted his horse to neigh.

"Good thing it's gettin' dark," Waco whispered.

A man came through the screen of brush, stopped his horse, and looked searchingly to the right and the left. Waco and Jim Barre, at the edge of the little opening in the brush, remained motionless. In such a manner does a wild thing hide from a hunter. The rider went back into the brush and out of sight, the sounds of his progress drifting back, fainter and fainter. When silence had descended once more, Waco released the grulla's head.

"An' now?" he said.

"Now," Jim voiced his partner's wish, "we'll head back. If they're lookin' for us, there won't be so many at the shack."

Waco lifted the mule's lead rope and, together, the men rode back toward the east, searching for the trail that they had followed not half an hour before.

Finding the trail, they traveled along it slowly, ears and eyes alert. Then, knowing that they had come far enough on horseback, they dismounted, tied the horses and the mule just off the trail, and went ahead on foot.

Where the trail entered the clearing, they stopped and listened. Peering through the growing dark, they could see the dim bulk of the house and of the corral behind it. There was no light, no sound, no sign of life.

"Suppose they all went out?" Waco whispered. "Mebbe they pulled their freight. Mebbe they. . . ." He stopped. There was a faint sound in the dark now, a low moaning that seemed to come from the house. It ceased and then came again, fainter than before.

"Somebody's in there," Jim whispered, and moved forward, Waco following.

They went stealthily across the clearing and, reaching the rock wall, stopped again. Once more the moaning had ceased. Now it came again, one long, piteous groan.

"I'm goin' in," Jim Barre whispered. "Watch the outside, Waco."

Four

Murder

Moving cautiously, Jim slipped forward. He reached the door of the rock house and, stopping, listened again. There was no sound or indication of life. Taking courage from the silence, Jim took two swift steps and was across the threshold and through the open door.

Here he waited a long time, listening, his eyes trying to penetrate the blackness. From his left there came a little sound — slow, sodden, steady — almost like the muted ticking of a great clock that was running down. The spaces between the sounds grew greater until, presently, there was no sound at all. Jim moved on the hard-packed dirt floor, shifting to the left. His extended foot struck something soundlessly, something that was soft and yielding.

Reaching into his pocket, Jim found a match. His gun was already in one hand. Striking the match against his thigh, he held it well away from him as it flamed, waiting for what the light might bring. Nothing happened.

Outside the door Waco whispered: "Jim?"

"All right," Jim answered, low-voiced. "Nobody here, Waco."

There was the sound of movement, and then Waco was beside his partner. The match flame made a little yellow spot of light in which Jim could see the thing his foot had struck — a leg covered by blue denim and terminating in a patched and worn boot. The match burned out.

Almost immediately another light flamed in Waco's hand. Now they could see the man who wore the boot. He lay upon

41

a bunk, tattered bed clothing tangled about him. His yellow face was battered almost beyond semblance to a face, and the lank, gray hair that crowned it was stained and matted with blood. Beside the edge of the bunk was a pool of blood, and, as the light reflected from its shining surface, one more drop fell, making the little sound that Jim had heard. The sickly flame of the match faded and died, and Waco let go his breath in one long gasp.

"Outside, Waco," Jim Barre said thickly. "Get outside." He moved toward the lighter blackness that was the door.

Standing near the rock wall outside the house, Waco close beside him, Jim Barre spoke again: "They beat him to death. It was him that yelled."

Waco grunted deeply in his chest.

"An' that's why they shot at us," Jim continued after a moment. "It was happenin' when we got here."

"But why?" demanded Waco.

"I wish I knew."

Silence came between the men. Jim Barre moved toward the entrance to the trail, and Waco followed noiselessly. When they reached their horses, they stopped.

"Now what, Jim?" Waco asked. As happened often, he turned to the younger man for direction.

"I think," Jim Barre said slowly, "that we'd ought to get word to the officers, Waco. That's what I think we'd better do."

"They shot at us," Waco reminded belligerently.

"An' we shot back." There was a little pause while Jim untied his horse. "An' anyhow," he said, "I've quit that business. I've quit it for keeps!" There was a savagery in his tone, a sudden harshness, and Waco, knowing its reason, did not argue. Instead, he reached for his bridle reins.

"There's a store down below Saunders," he suggested.

"That would be the nearest place to go."

"Then," growled Jim, "let's go there."

Both men mounted, and Waco took the mule's lead rope. Silently they rode down the trail and, skirting the clearing wherein stood the silent cabin, entered a trail that led out on the other side. For half an hour they rode slowly, the trail gradually bending northward. Then Jim reined in.

"Too dark to go on for now," he said. "We'd just get lost. We'll stop here, Waco."

"It'll be moonlight pretty soon," Waco pointed out.

"We don't know the country," insisted Jim. "I think we'd better stop now."

Waco gave consent by stopping and dismounting.

In the morning, with the first gray light, they went on. As the light grew, Waco could take his landmarks from the Chisos, and angled sharply from the trail toward the north. Within three miles they struck a wagon road and, following it, came, as the sun rose, to a little settlement.

There was a two-story building with a battered sign across its front that proclaimed it was a store. Beyond the store a little rock house squatted, and to its east was a cluster of adobe houses. Trees — leafless now — marched in a narrow line, telling plainly of the presence of running water, and beneath the trees the white of tents showed.

"Gaskin's Crossroads," Waco said and looked at his companion.

It was almost the first word spoken since they had left their camp that morning. Jim Barre's face was worn and savage beneath his stubble of beard. He nodded in answer to the statement, but made no verbal response.

From the tents beside the creek a horseman detached himself and came riding toward the store, approaching it from one angle, while Waco and Jim Barre came from another. The rider reached the store and stopped, dismounting and tying his horse to the deserted hitch rail. Jim gave a little grunt of surprise as the man turned, and urged his horse to a quicker pace. Waco kept up, and the unwilling mule overcame her reluctance and broke into a trot. As the two reined in beside the hitch rack, the rider from the creek stepped forward, a tall, gaunt figure of a man with gray hair and mustache.

A smile lighted the face of the newcomer as he reached up his hand toward Jim Barre. "Jim" — the voice was deep and slow, with a ring of authority — "I'm glad to see you."

"An' I'm glad to see *you*, Captain." Jim Barre bent down to take the extended hand. "Mighty glad."

For an instant the hands locked and held. Then, releasing his grip, Jim straightened and looked at Waco.

"This is Waco Ibolt, Captain," he said. "Waco, shake hands with Captain Ringold."

Obediently Waco extended his hand, and Ringold took it. "I've heard of you, Ibolt," he said, smiling.

"An' I heard of you," Waco replied with emphasis. "I reckon everybody in Texas knows about Cap'n Nate Ringold of the rangers."

Greetings over, Ringold settled his broad shoulders against the post at one end of the hitch rail, and smiled at Jim Barre.

"What are you doin' in this country, Jim?" he asked. "I thought you were goin' to stay over west, around El Paso."

"We came down wolfin'," Jim explained. "It was Waco's idea. An' last night we run into somethin'."

He continued then, outlining briefly the happenings at the rock house. Waco interposed a word or two, and Ringold listened, his eyes narrowed as he nodded his head occasionally.

"I'll go back there with you," he announced when the recital was finished. "I just came in here with my company yesterday. We were ordered down from the north. And I want to talk to you, Jim. I've got something on my mind. Have you boys had breakfast?"

"We ain't et since yesterday noon," Waco answered promptly. "I'm gettin' pretty ga'nt."

"You go over to camp," Ringold ordered. "We've had breakfast, but the cook will fix you up. There's boys over there that you know, Jim, an' I reckon they won't run you off." He smiled easily. "I'll go into the store an' talk to Thad Gaskin for a minute, an' then I'll join you."

For an instant after the ranger's departure, Waco stood looking at the empty door, then, turning to his horse, he twisted out a stirrup.

"Ain't that luck?" he said. "Now ain't that luck to find *him* here?"

As Ringold had said, Jim Barre was acquainted with some of the men in the ranger camp. When he had introduced Waco and had, himself, met the others of the ten men who comprised Nate Ringold's company, they squatted beside the fire, eating, drinking coffee, and awaiting the return of the officer. The men were friendly, but they did not ask questions, and Waco and Jim Barre withheld their own natural curiosity. The rangers had come on business. What that business was might or might not be divulged, according to Ringold's wishes.

The captain, returning, dismounted and joined the group at the fire. Waco wiped the last of the bacon grease from his lips, and Jim Barre, putting his cup and plate in the wreck pan, joined the officer.

"You ready?" Ringold asked, and, when Jim assented, the tall man drawled orders. "We got some spare horses for once. You boys better take two of 'em."

A ranger private on horse guard hurried away to bring in the stock, and Ringold, leading his sergeant aside, spoke briefly. Fresh mounts were roped out for Waco and Jim, and two rangers, at their captain's orders, also saddled horses. Within ten minutes of Ringold's return, the little party was striking along the wagon road, riding south.

Jim Barre rode beside Ringold. For a while there was silence between them, and then the ranger captain drawled pleasant inquiry concerning Jim's work and general well-being. Jim answered freely. This was a preliminary round, the men sparring. Ringold had something on his mind, something pressing, and Jim knew it. Suddenly the captain struck the first real blow.

"Jim," he said levelly, "I want you to go to work for me again."

Barre had known that this was coming, and yet he could not avoid it. He turned his head, meeting Ringold's level eyes, and answered: "No, Captain."

"I knew you'd say that," Ringold stated. "But I'm not done. Let me talk. You were a corporal with me when you had your tough luck. I think I know you, Jim, and I know how you feel. But this is bigger than you or me."

Jim Barre waited, and Ringold, collecting his thoughts, went on: "I've been sent down here, and every other ranger command is spotted along the border from El Paso to Brownsville." He paused again, looking at Jim Barre to see if his words were making an impression. "We've had word," he continued, "that old Porfirio Díaz is on the way out over in Mexico. He's run that country a long time, and they're tired of him. They're goin' to kick him out. And when they do, there'll be hell along the border, Jim, and that's why the rangers are down here."

Jim looked straight ahead. He knew that what Ringold said

was true, providing always that Mexico was, indeed, done with Porfirio Díaz. The old man had ruled with an iron hand, and his *Rurales* kept order; but with Díaz gone, the old days of swift raids into Texas, of raping and murder and bloodshed, would return. The rangers were needed along the border.

"I've got ten men," Ringold continued. "After the trouble starts, I'll be allowed more, but ten is my limit now. I've got to keep them together so that I can hit full force where I'm needed. And I've got to have scouts out ahead, Jim. Men that I can trust and that will know what's going on. That's why I need you."

This also was true, Jim Barre thought. Ringold must be in the center of the circle, able to strike along its radii, and, at the edge of the circle, he must have his informants, men that he could trust, men who would watch and bring him word. Only so might catastrophe be avoided. But still Jim did not answer.

Ringold's voice lowered a tone, and the words came softly. "You worked for me one time," he drawled. "I sent you out to arrest a man that had been your friend. I didn't know that at the time, and you didn't tell me. You thought that you could bring him in without trouble. That's why you went. You had to kill him. I didn't blame you when you quit. I might have done the same. You told me that you were through then, that you'd never be a ranger again. You were a good ranger, and I hated to see you go, but I let you. Now I need you. Can you turn me down?"

Jim Barre wavered in his decision. He looked keenly at the tall, gray-haired man beside him and asked a question. "What about Waco?"

Ringold's voice was brisk. "Good," he said. "I knew you'd come through. I'll take Waco. You vouch for him, and I've heard of him. He's a good man. I can't pay you now, but,

47

when our appropriation goes through, I'll put you both on the muster list. You. . . ."

"I haven't said I would, Captain," Jim Barre interrupted.

"But you will," Ringold told him. "Now what I want you to do is this . . . go ahead with your trappin'. String a line of traps along the river an' cover them. Make friends down there. Wolvers won't be bothered, and you'll hear things an' see 'em. Then report to me. You'll do it, Jim?"

Jim Barre nodded slowly. "I'll do it," he agreed. "But you'll have to talk to Waco."

"I will," Ringold assured him. "He. . . ."

Behind them Waco called: "You're goin' to pass the turn-off, Jim. The trail's right ahead."

Roused from his thoughts by Waco's call, Jim Barre became aware of his surroundings again. They were almost abreast of the trail that led to the rock house.

Five

Ringold Asks Some Questions

When they reached the rock house, riding in boldly and in force, they found it deserted. There were no horses in the corral; nothing that spoke of a tenant. When Barre and Ringold entered the single room, they found it, too, deserted. Only the dried blood on the floor and the tangled, bloodied bedding on the bunk vouched for the truth of Jim Barre's tale. Ringold stood with inscrutable eyes, examining the room, while the rangers and Waco scouted the edge of the clearing, searching for tracks.

"They came back an' got him," Ringold stated. "Likely dumped him in the river. It ain't far off. Then they pulled their freight."

Waco and one ranger private appeared at the door.

"Plenty of sign, Cap'n," the ranger announced. "There's been a bunch of horses pulled out of here, headed south. Fresh tracks, too."

Ringold nodded. "Headed for the border," he announced. "No use in wastin' time here. Sam, you an' Frank follow those tracks an' see if they don't go to the river. Report back to camp. We'll go there now. Jim, you saw those men, didn't you?"

"Two of them," Jim replied. "Waco and I both saw the two that came out, an' we saw the dead man."

Ringold pondered a moment. "You'll describe them to Gaskin at the store," he said. "Old Thad knows everybody in the country. If they lived around here, he'll know 'em."

They walked out of the little room. The two ranger privates were mounted and already making toward the south edge of the clearing. Waco stood, holding the horses, frowning a little because he felt he did not fit in the group.

"You'll have to talk to Waco," Jim said again, his voice low.

Ringold nodded. "We'll ride back to camp," he said cheerfully. "There's nothin' here for us."

Returning along the trail, Jim fell back, allowing Waco to ride beside the ranger captain. Ringold's voice — low, the words indistinct — came back to him as the ranger talked to Waco, and, as they reached the road, Jim saw Waco nod agreement. It was settled, then. Waco had agreed to Ringold's proposal. Jim urged his horse ahead, for there was now room on the road for the men to ride three abreast.

"Waco," Ringold drawled, "thinks it's all right."

Jim Barre glanced across the neck of the captain's horse. Waco grinned at him and, perforce, Jim smiled back. Waco was all right. He was a hand. He wore a gun and knew how to use it, and he had an inflexible courage. But Waco didn't know. . . . The smile faded from Jim Barre's face, and he stared moodily at his horse's ears.

When they reached the crossroads, the three men went directly to the store. It was mid-afternoon, and the hitch rail was deserted. Dismounting, they left their horses and went into the store, Ringold in the lead.

A man, short, wiry, and tough as a rawhide hobble, came along the counter toward them, and in the back of the store, behind a high bookkeeper's desk, Jim could see a dark head bent. The head lifted as their boots thumped on the floor, and a thrill shot through Jim. Marilee Clark was standing behind the desk. Waco also saw the girl, and he grunted. It was evident that, looking against the light, she did not recognize the men. She lowered her head to her work again.

Ringold made the introductions. Waco Ibolt and Jim Barre shook hands with Thad Gaskin.

"They're goin' to trap wolves down below in the Chisos," the ranger explained. "Likely you can sell 'em a bill of goods, Gaskin."

Gaskin's smile was dry. "They's plenty of wolves to trap," he commented.

"An' they ran into somethin' comin' in here," Ringold proceeded. "Let's step outside, Thad."

The storekeeper raised curious eyes to the captain's face, but obeyed the suggestion. Outside the store on the shaded porch, Ringold squatted beside the wall. Waco joined him there, while Gaskin sat on a box and Jim Barre leaned against the porch support.

"Tell him, Jim," Ringold ordered. "All of it. Thad's all right, and he can keep his mouth shut."

The storekeeper, drawing a knife from his pocket, split off a long sliver from the box on which he sat, and Jim Barre, laconically, but omitting no detail, told his story. When he had finished, all three looked at the storekeeper, who continued to whittle.

"That man," Gaskin said suddenly, "was Chino Joe. He was a half-breed . . . Chinese and Mexican. The two men you saw were the Lemoine brothers. I have no idea who was with 'em."

"How do you know about the half-breed?" Ringold demanded.

"Because" — Gaskin looked up from his whittling — "he's the only one that's ever been in this country. His father came here to cook for Howie Clark an' married a Mexican woman. Joe was with Howie when he was killed over across the river two years ago." The storekeeper peeled off a long sliver of wood, watched it drop, and then looked up again. "And I can tell you why he was killed," he added quietly.

"Why?" Ringold's voice was sharp.

"Because," Gaskin said, "Howie Clark was supposed to have found a gold mine before he was killed, an' because the Lemoines have been tryin' to find that mine. They've been lookin' for Chino Joe ever since he pulled out, right after Howie was killed."

"You mean Chino Joe's been gone?" Ringold asked.

Gaskin nodded. "For two years," he agreed. "He pulled out right after Howie was murdered. Some folks thought he did it, but he brought the body back, an' it's been pretty well proved now that Howie was killed by Agapito de Griego's bunch. Leastwise, they bragged about it."

"An' Chino Joe was supposed to know where the mine was located?" Waco asked curiously.

"He was." Gaskin favored his questioner with a long stare. "He came back with Howie Clark's body an' ridin' Howie's horse. He had a wild tale about somethin' that Howie had told him before he died. Somethin' about Howie's saddle bein' valuable an' that he was to give it to Howie's kids. There was quite a lot of talk, an' some hotheads was goin' to lynch Joe for the murder. He sloped out one night, and I don't blame him. I didn't know he'd come back to this country." Again Gaskin's knife bit into the soft wood. "Dale an' Marilee Clark were gone when their father was killed," he said softly, looking at the wood.

"Dale Clark was Howie's son?" Jim Barre blurted the question. "An' Marilee his daughter?"

Gaskin's eyes were sharp as he looked at Jim. "Did you know Dale?"

"I punched cows with him," Jim answered. "We were in Carver City when he was killed. I saw Marilee . . . Miss Clark . . . an' tried to help her."

For the first time a tinge of warmth came into Gaskin's eyes. "The poor kid," he said.

A little pause followed, and then Ringold asked a question: "These Lemoines. What about them?"

"Carl an' Fox Lemoine," Gaskin said. "They're bad. They worked for Tayler an' Clark when Clark was killed, an' they know about the mine Clark was supposed to have found. They've been lookin' for it ever since, what time they haven't been stealin' cattle or into some other devilment. It was too bad that Chino Joe run into them."

"Clark had a ranch here?" Waco could not restrain his natural curiosity.

"Clark and a man named Tayler," Gaskin answered shortly. "Tayler's got it now."

"But if Clark had two kids . . . ?" Waco began.

"Tayler had bought Clark out before Clark was killed," Gaskin said, his voice curt. "He had the papers to prove it, but Howie Clark never left a cent of money. If you want to know about that, you'll have to ask Tayler. He don't come here!" The storekeeper closed his knife with a snap. Evidently this was a sore subject and one to be avoided.

Ringold pushed himself up from where he squatted. "Thanks, Thad," he drawled. "At least, we know who was killed an' some of them that done it. You boys" — he looked at Jim and Waco — "will kind of know who to watch out for now."

"Who owns that country in the Chisos?" Jim Barre asked.

"Tayler." Gaskin got up from his box. "He won't mind your trappin'. Anyhow, I don't think he will. Did you have any more questions? I've told you what I know."

"No more questions," Ringold said. "Jim, you an' Waco will throw down with us tonight. Then tomorrow you can start out. I think. . . ."

He did not finish the sentence. Marilee Clark, pushing open the door, came out on the porch.

"Uncle Thad," she began, and then, seeing the others, stopped, confused.

Thad Gaskin took a step and stood beside the girl protectively. "This is Captain Ringold, Marilee," he said. "An' yon's Mister Barre an' Mister Ibolt, friends of the captain's."

A smile lit the girl's face, and her eyes searched Jim's face. "I think I've met Mister Barre," she said. "And I'm very glad to meet you, Captain, and Mister Ibolt."

Waco's face was red beneath its tan. Jim Barre stared at the girl, and, then, he also flushed hotly, suddenly aware that he was being rude.

"You had somethin' to ask me, Marilee?" Gaskin said.

"I wanted to know about an entry you made while I was gone," the girl answered, and, smiling at the others, moved toward the door.

"I'll be there in a minute," Gaskin said. As the girl went on into the store, he turned to Ringold and his companions. "You'll be around this country," he announced. "Anyway I can help you, I'll be glad to do it. An' if you two have some skins to sell, I'll make you a price on 'em." He nodded briskly to Waco and Jim, and walked to the door.

"We'll see you, Thad," Ringold said, and started down the steps.

Waco, following the ranger captain, paused on the top step. "When does the mail come out?" he asked Gaskin. "I see you got a post office an'. . . ."

"Every day except Sunday," Gaskin interrupted curtly. "It comes down from Saunders on a star route. Gets here at noon an' goes right back. If you get any letters, I'll hold 'em, an', if a telegram comes, the agent at Saunders will send it down. You expectin' a message?"

"No," Waco answered, his curiosity satisfied. "I just wanted to know."

Gaskin grunted and went into the store.

Six

Laying Traps

Waco, kneeling on a square of canvas, dirt piled beside him and heavy leather gloves on his hands, looked up and grinned at Jim Barre. Jim rested his elbow on the flat horn of the Mexican saddle and surveyed his partner's handiwork with interest.

"I learned this," Waco announced, "in Montana. If it works up there, it ought to work down here." Carefully he placed the Number 4½ Newhouse trap in the hole that he had dug, coiled the chain and drag hook in place, and put the leather trap pad between the jaws. Tipping back on his boot heels, he squinted at his artistry. "It's all in knowin' how," he stated, "an' in usin' no iron to work with. A wolf hates iron, an' he can sure smell it."

"The trap's got iron in it," Jim objected. "If a wolf can smell so blamed good, how come you can use an iron trap?"

"They don't make traps out of cheese," Waco answered. "Anyhow, this trap's been rubbed good with beef tallow, an' smoked. That'll smell like dinner to a wolf. An', besides, when I git done he ain't goin' to be worried about no trap nohow."

With a wooden trowel he began cautiously to ladle dirt over the trap jaws and the wide pad. "Put the dirt on the canvas," he said, "an' cart it off with you, so they won't see nothin' wrong. Use gloves to work with, an' keep 'em tallowed. Don't walk around. Just drop your canvas an' get off your horse on it. That's kindergarten stuff in wolf trappin'. You got to do all that, an' you got to know where to set your trap." He sprinkled dust from the trowel over the

56

now concealed trap, added a little more, and got up.

"An' how do you know where to set your trap?" Jim Barre asked politely.

"You learn." Waco faced around. "This here is a wolf whistlin' post, like on the railroad. This is where they come an' call. They got regular stops all around the country they're usin', an', when they hit one, they stop an' smell, an' then leave their sign. Smellin' tells 'em who's been there an' what's happenin'. Wolves can leave a message, I reckon. After we've caught a few, they'll all know it an' then's when the trappin' gets tough. Now pass me that bottle I give you. I'm goin' to play wolf an' leave some sign myself."

With a grimace of disgust Jim Barre passed over the bottle he carried. Waco shook the bottle, uncorked it, and splashed a portion of its contents on the little clump of bear grass beside the trap. "There!" he said, corking the bottle. "Mister Wolf will think the old man coyote done come along, when he smells that." He looked up at Jim, noted his utter disbelief, and grinned again.

"When you killed that coyote, you thought I was crazy to empty his bladder in a bottle," Waco observed. "This here's what I done it for. Now we'll go. We got some more traps to set."

Stepping from the canvas, he gathered it up carefully so that the dirt would not spill, and held it up to Jim. Then, relieved of his burden, he mounted Oscar, took off his hat, and, bending, swept the hat back and forth a time or two, fanning out the tracks of his boots.

"An' if that don't catch a wolf, I'll be surprised," Waco announced. "Come on, Jim."

When they had ridden off some distance, Jim, at Waco's direction, dumped the dirt out of the canvas and, folding the cloth, tied it to his saddle.

"All that work to set a trap," Jim scoffed as they rode on once more. "You'd think the wolves were smart as a man."

"They are, pretty near," Waco said seriously. "Long time back . . . oh, mebbe ten years ago . . . they was foolish. You could trap 'em just 'most any way, an' they went for poison. We used to set a line of posts an' bore holes in 'em an' fill the holes with tallow an' strychnine. The wolves an' coyotes would lick it out, an' it would kill 'em. Then the wolves got scarce, an' nobody trapped, an' all of a sudden they was back again, smart old lobos that you couldn't hardly ketch. It takes a lot of brains to trap a wolf nowadays. You wasn't wrong when you said that they was smart as a man."

"Go on, teacher," Jim Barre gibed. "Hand out the rest of it."

Waco disregarded the raillery in the tone and words. He was launched on his favorite subject, and he expounded cheerfully. "This spring," he said, "we'll find some dens an' get 'em that way. Lots of times you can get five or six pups in a den."

"Trap 'em?" Jim asked.

"Shoot 'em," Waco answered. "That's why I got this rifle." He slapped the stock of his saddle gun projecting in front of his right thigh.

"So that's why you're carryin' that cannon," Jim said.

"That's why," Waco agreed. "A Winchester Thirty-Thirty is all right for a saddle gun. It's handy an' a lot easier to carry than this one is. But when it comes to shootin' three hundred yards an' bringin' home the bacon, I'll take a Krag. The magazine makes it unhandy as the devil to carry on a saddle, but it sure shoots. You can lay off from a den with this an' shoot the ol' dog wolf while he's hangin' around, an' then get the she-wolf an' the pups."

"An' where are we goin' now?" Jim asked.

"There's an old dead cow about two miles from here," Waco answered. "I thought we'd put some traps around her. She's too rotten for a wolf to eat, but they like to roll on somethin' like that, an', if we make a set there, we'll likely get one."

"Lead on to your dead cow," Jim said grimly. "If you can stand the smell, I can."

They set four traps beside the carcass that Waco had located, Jim doing the setting under the critical instruction of his companion. Then they set a trap where a trail, passable only for wolves or coyotes or goats, broke over the edge of the cañon that dropped, sheer and steep, five hundred feet toward the Río Grande. Waco picked the spots and did most of the setting. When evening came, they had placed the last of the fifteen traps they had brought.

"An' now," Waco said, "we'll head for home an' supper. Tomorrow we'll go the other way an' set that line of traps."

Home was a shack built partly of rocks, partly of thin poles, planted in a double line, and the space between them filled with hard-packed mud. Waco and Jim Barre had found the shack when they had explored the foothills of the Chisos. It was perhaps a quarter of a mile north of the river, and a seep of water from the hill behind it insured a supply for drinking. The Río Grande itself ran deeply in a gorge, and a trail led down that steep slope, a trail that a burro or a man on foot might travel.

Close by the *jacal* the original builder had constructed a corral from ocotillo stems, and this served well enough when the partners wished to pen their stock. For the most part, however, Oscar and Monte, and the mule, Blanca, were turned loose with hobbles. There was sufficient grass for them, and a plenitude of mesquite beans upon which the mule would grow fat. Firewood there was, too, in abundance, and while the cooking arrangements were primitive — consisting solely of an open hearth and fireplace — the house suited their purpose.

The only drawback to the location was its proximity to the rock house where the half-breed had been killed. That camp was not more than five miles distant, north and west of them. Jim Barre, discussing this fact with Waco, had found that the little man rather liked the idea of being close to the other house. Waco was combative, and he had not forgotten the swift attack upon himself and his friend. Nor would he soon forget the half-breed's death.

"Mebbe they'll use that place again sometime," Waco had grated when he and Jim discussed the location of their camp. "I kind of hope they do."

Secretly Jim had felt a good deal the same way, and so they had thrown a few shovels full of dirt on the roof of the *jacal*, patching the thin places, swept out the interior with a cedar branch, killed some centipedes brought to life by the heat of the fire, and moved in.

Returning from setting their first line of traps, Waco and Jim pushed open the sagging door, dumped saddles, bridles, and blankets down on the hard-packed dirt floor, and were at home. Waco built a fire in the fireplace, and Jim took a bucket to the seep for water.

When Jim returned, the fire was blazing cheerfully, and Waco had salt pork bubbling in the pan. Supper eaten, the few dishes washed and cigarettes rolled and lighted, the men lounged on their beds, Waco expounding on the habits of wolves, and Jim listening with interest. The fire died, and Waco got up from his box and split slivers of cedar with his axe to make kindling for the morning fire. This was the last act of the night, and Jim, seated on his bed, began to pull off his boots.

"Tomorrow, early," Waco announced, "you ride the line we set today, an' I'll take the east side an' set it. That way, we'll kind of take care of things."

Jim nodded. He was pleasantly tired, and he stretched out in his blankets.

"An'," said Waco, "once we get this trap line set, we'll have some time to tend to Ringold's business for him. Good night, Jim."

"Good night," Jim responded sleepily. He heard Waco groan and stretch. A chunk of wood snapped in the fireplace, and then all was still.

In the morning, shivering from the chill of the room, Jim built the fire. Waco heated the cold biscuits in the Dutch oven and made the coffee, complaining against his lack of foresight concerning the coffee supply, which was almost exhausted. With breakfast eaten, they went out, caught the horses, and rode away — one toward the east, the other west.

There were no wolves in the traps that Jim first visited. Sign was plentiful, but the makers of the sign had passed by the traps. Not until he came to the trap at the sign post, did Jim have any luck. There the trap was gone, and there was a trail into the brush showing where the animal had dragged the trap.

Jim followed the trail and within two hundred yards found both the trap and its captive, a half-grown wolf that faced him defiantly, teeth bared viciously. Jim killed the wolf and sprang the trap. Then, squatting, he flayed the pelt from the body, rolled it, and carried it to Monte, who snorted and rolled his eyes. It took a good deal of persuasion for Jim to get close to the horse. Monte was imbued with a profound distaste for wolf, and he did his best to manifest it. Finally the horse was calmed, and, carrying the jangling trap and hide,

Jim rode on. He must, he thought, find a new site for that trap.

He found it — another sign post, the place made plain by the numerous tracks. Here, dropping his canvas, Jim dismounted, hobbled Monte, and set about preparing a trap site as he had been instructed. When the trap was in place, he gathered up the canvas, mounted, and then rode on.

At the trap he had set under Waco's supervision, Jim found something new. A wolf, very evidently aware that there was a trap located at the spot, had stopped and contemptuously scratched rock and gravel over the place. Other signs of the animal's contempt were in evidence also, and Jim Barre could not keep from laughing.

"Knew I was an amateur, didn't you?" he remarked to the absent wolf, and, dismounting, picked up the trap. He would set it again, perhaps with better luck.

By noon Jim had finished his ride, the solitary pelt the only fruit of his endeavor. Returning to the cabin, he avoided riding directly along the trap line, staying well away, and yet in sight of it. When he reached the camp, Waco had not come in, and so, hobbling Monte and turning him out to graze, Jim went into the house, washed the breakfast dishes, and put the place to rights. When he looked at the almost empty coffee can, he grinned. Waco liked coffee and would not get along without it. That coffee can was going to be an excuse to ride to Gaskin's Corners some day soon.

Waco came in late, tired and hungry. He had set his line of traps, and, while he ate the supper Jim had waiting for him, the little man recounted his experiences of the day. He had gone east and, about fifteen miles in that direction, he reported, there was a town.

"Ain't much," Waco said. "Just a *pueblito* named Pajaritos. There's two, three houses an' a creek that goes

62

down to the river. I stopped and visited around a while. Kind of friendly people. The feller I talked to was named Sanchez. He give me a taste of the hottest chili I ever threw a lip over."

"Didn't find out anything?" Jim asked.

"Not a thing. They got some goats, an' I seen some jerky on poles. I don't think the jerky come from their goats. There's a good trail down to the river there. Follows the creek. It's a place we're goin' to have to watch, Jim."

"There's two or three trails on my side," Jim Barre said. "Just cow tracks. I don't think anybody could use 'em."

"Where a cow can go, a horse can foller," Waco quoted. "We'll watch all along here, Jim. Tomorrow I'll take you down the line I set today, so you'll know where the traps are. An' you can get a look at Pajaritos. How about it?"

"All right," Jim agreed. "I guess I could stand some more lessons. I ain't exactly what you'd call a success at trappin', Waco." He went on then, telling of the trap the wolf had scorned.

Waco laughed heartily. "I told you they was smart," he reminded when he had finished. "Tell you what. We'll ride your line in the mornin' an' take mine in the afternoon."

And that was the program. The following morning, as Waco had said, they rode Jim's line of traps. One had been sprung, but the animal — wolf, coyote, civet cat, or whatever it was — had gotten away. That trap Jim reset under Waco's direction. The other traps had not been touched.

In the afternoon, riding Waco's line of traps, they found and killed two wolves. These they skinned. Being so delayed, they did not reach Waco's discovery until almost four o'clock. Side by side, they rode down the slope of the *pueblito* set beside the creek.

The rock houses were small, and, as Waco had said, the inhabitants of the houses ran goats. The odor itself was enough to advise Jim of that fact, even had he not seen a small herd of bearded animals working on a hillside above the little settlement.

Manuel Sanchez, loafing in front of his house, greeted Waco placidly, not moving from where he sat. Pigeons fluttered all about the place, perching on roofs or on the ground, flying out on short excursions from the dovecote that stood on the roof of Manuel's house.

Sanchez accepted tobacco and papers, and spoke gentle Spanish, while round-eyed little boys and girls, clothed only in skimpy upper garments, peered from doorways and windows at *los gringos*.

No, Sanchez said, there was no one that went across the river. Not many followed the trail. Oh, sometimes — he shrugged — one could hear travelers at night, but these were very few of late and, *por diablos,* a man was busy with his own business and not that of others. What did the *señores* think of his goats? Were they not fine animals? And the price of mohair was good. Must the *señores* go? *"Vaya con Dios."*

"He's so danged lazy he wouldn't turn over if he was lyin' on a cactus," Waco observed as he and Jim rode back together up the hill. "He don't know a thing, an' does less."

Jim Barre thought about that, and then shook his head. "I ain't so sure," he answered. "He's lazy, yeah, but he's stout as a bull. An' I got a look inside his house. He's got a Winchester standin' by the door, an' it's in good shape. You can't ever tell about a Mexican, Waco. You ought to know that."

"I can tell about *him*," Waco answered. "He runs goats. You can smell 'em on him."

When the two rode down into the valley that contained the little camp, dark had come. Brush and rocks were dim shapes that loomed ominously in the distance and then, as they drew close, resolved into brush and rocks. The men did not talk now as they rode, and their horses made a steady plopping sound as they walked. Suddenly Jim Barre, in the lead, reined in sharply, and Waco stopped beside him. Down in the camp a light winked brightly.

"Company," Jim Barre said. "Now who . . . ?" He checked. There was a moment's silence, and then Waco spoke.

"The way to find out is to ride in, Jim."

"An' so we'll do that," Jim agreed.

Seven

Stupe Wadell

The advance to the shack was not so simple as Waco had outlined. Both Waco and Jim were wary men, and this was the Big Bend, where wariness paid dividends in continued living. Before they reached the shack, they dismounted, and Waco pulled the Krag-Jorgensen carbine from his saddle boot. That insurance taken, Jim strode ahead, keeping out of line with the shack's door, while his partner hovered watchfully beside the horses.

Before Jim reached the door, it opened, and a man stood outlined by the light behind him in the doorway.

Jim called — "Hello!" — and came on, his caution dropped.

Waco, too, advanced, leading the horses.

The man in the doorway stepped out and stood waiting. "You the fellows that are camped here?" he demanded when Jim came up.

"Yes," Jim agreed. "We're wolfin' along the river."

Waco, leaving the horses beside the corral fence, joined his partner. "Howdy," he said brusquely.

"Howdy." The stranger was as brusque as Waco.

"Come in," Jim invited. "I see you built a fire."

The stranger stepped into the shack, Waco and Jim filing in behind him. In the little room the man faced around. "My name's Tayler," he stated. "I run cattle over this country."

"Pleased to meet you," Jim said. "My name's Barre. This is my partner, Waco Ibolt."

Tayler made no move to shake hands. Waco crossed over to the corner and dumped down the pelts he carried. The ranchman did not watch Waco, but continued to stare at Jim.

"Wolfin', are you?" he said. "It's kind of usual for a wolfer to drop in an' mention it when he's trappin' a man's country."

This was true. Tayler had put Jim at a disadvantage.

Jim nodded. "We'd been plannin' to do it, too. We've just been here two days." He was slightly apologetic.

There was movement outside the door. Monte, a biscuit eater if ever there was one, appeared beyond the opening, his wise buckskin head almost inside the shack. Waco yelled at the horse and lifted his arm threateningly, and Monte backed out, swinging around as he cleared the door, showing his side and then his buckskin hips. Jim turned back to Tayler as the horse disappeared.

Suddenly Tayler smiled. "No harm done," he said. "I'm glad to have you here. I've been losin' stock to the wolves. When I came along here this evenin', I saw somebody was usin' the place, so I stopped. Naturally I'm interested in who is in my country."

"I don't blame you for that," Jim said. "An' we should have come over to your headquarters an' asked you if it was all right for us to locate here."

Waco put wood on the fire and drew a frying pan toward him. "We'll have supper in a minute," he announced. "You'll eat with us, Mister Tayler?"

"An' you'd better stay the night," Jim suggested, trying to make up for the mistake by proffering hospitality.

Tayler smiled, his lips parting beneath his black mustache, his gray-green eyes flitting constantly from Jim to Waco and back again.

"I'll eat supper, but I won't stay the night," he answered. "I've got to be at the north end of the ranch early tomorrow, so I'll have to go home tonight."

"You unsaddle the horses while I get supper," Waco directed, looking at Jim. "We sure overlooked our hand in not comin' to you before this, Mister Tayler, but mebbe we'll make up for it. We already got three wolves."

Jim went on out, leaving Tayler talking with Waco.

When he returned, the odor of frying bacon assailed his nostrils, and Waco had the Dutch oven on the coals. Tayler had squatted down beside the wall and was telling Waco about a big lobo that had been killing cattle almost at his headquarters. Dumping the Mexican saddle down beside the door, Jim joined the conversation.

The talk during the simple meal was brief and casual. Tayler spoke of range conditions, mentioned the fact that he had seen more wolf sign farther north than he had along the river, and suggested that the partners try trapping up in that direction. Waco assured the rancher that they would take his advice as soon as they had worked the immediate country, and Tayler told them of a camp up at the north end that the two could use.

The meal over, Tayler rolled a cigarette and made ready to leave. "I hate to eat an' run," he said, "but you see how it is? The moon's up, an' I'd better be goin'."

Both Waco and Jim Barre again pressed him to stay, but Tayler quietly refused. Accompanying him out to his horse, the partners saw the rancher mount and ride away.

When they returned to the shack, Waco spoke. "Seems like a pretty decent sort of gent, don't he?"

Jim nodded. "We should have dropped in an' asked him if it was all right for us to trap," he said. "I don't know why we didn't."

Waco curled brown paper about tobacco. Above the forming cigarette he looked quizzically at his friend. "I'll tell you somethin' you don't know," he drawled. "He's the gent that bought your saddle."

The statement came with the suddenness of a lightning bolt. Jim Barre gaped, open-mouthed, at his partner. "Why didn't you say so?" he demanded. "You. . . ."

Waco lighted the smoke he had rolled. "*He* didn't mention it, did he?" the little man drawled.

"No. But . . . ?"

"Then who was I to go bringin' it up? Mebbe he wanted to forget about it. How do I know? Mebbe he was so drunk when he made the deal that he didn't know he done it. Anyhow, I wasn't goin' to go pryin' around. He was sore enough at us the way it was."

Jim considered Waco's statement. "He was sore when he came in," he said. "An' then he cleared right up an' was friendly as a basket of chips. But why didn't he say somethin'? He must've known you."

"Mebbe he knew me, mebbe he didn't," Waco said. "It's a cinch, if he did know me, he kept mighty still about it."

"But why?" Jim asked again.

"Oh, hell!" Waco dismissed the subject. "He was sore because we didn't ask him could we trap, an' then, when he found out we were doin' all right, he got over it. He wants the wolves cleaned off his range. That's all. Forget it, Jim. One of these days, when we kind of get acquainted, we'll all hurrah each other about that saddle deal. He looks like a nice sort of fellow. Come on, let's wash the dishes."

Reluctantly Jim took a dish towel from a peg. "I sure don't get it," he said. "An' I'll tell you somethin' else I don't get, Waco. That must be his camp where the half-breed was killed, and still he didn't say a thing about it."

"Mebbe he don't know about it." Waco put a washed plate on the table.

"Mebbe he don't." Jim picked up the plate. "But if he

don't, he's the only one in the country who doesn't. I tell you, Waco, this is a funny deal, all the way through."

"Funny or not, he's the fellow that bought your saddle."

They continued to talk while they washed the dishes, discussing their recent visitor, considering various angles of the visit. The last dish dried, Waco made one final statement.

"Anyhow, he was all clouded up when we came in, an' it wasn't till that buckskin pie biter of yours tried to get in the door that he turned friendly. I reckon we got Monte to thank for him not runnin' us off." Having delivered this statement, Waco picked up the dishes and turned to put them on the shelves of the box cupboard fastened to the wall. "An' I'll tell you somethin' else," he said, turning from the cupboard. "We're out of coffee an' matches an' we're pretty near out of bakin' powder. We'll have to go to Gaskin's an' get some tomorrow."

"All right," Jim agreed absently. "We'll do it."

They rode their trap lines the following morning, Waco using the mule as a means of transportation. Both the horses, under the steady riding, were gaunting and showed that they needed rest or grain, or both. Accordingly, the mule was pressed into service, her rider decided by flipping a coin. When, shortly after noon, the two men returned to the camp, both were laden. Waco had two pelts, and Jim had taken two coyotes and a wolf in his traps. Both were frankly elated, and Waco indulged in a little crowing and a few I-told-you-sos.

So many skins to care for altered their plans. They had, that morning, decided that they would go to the Crossroads together, but now Waco vetoed that idea. He would stay and flesh the pelts and spread them, he said. Jim could go to the store for the supplies.

Jim demurred. He did not want to leave the work to Waco,

70

but the little man was insistent, claiming that he knew more about the preparation of fur than did his partner, and also stating plainly that he wasn't going to get along without coffee. So, after a hasty lunch, Jim saddled Monte and set out.

Looking back at the little camp as he rode away, Jim could see Waco in the doorway. The small man waved, and Jim lifted his hand in answer. Despite the fact that Waco himself had chosen to stay at the camp, Jim felt a sense of guilt. He wished that Waco had come along. There weren't many like Waco. Not many partners would have stayed at home and worked while the other went tramping off to town. A mighty good little man, Waco Ibolt.

When Jim reached the Crossroads and stopped in front of Gaskin's, he found another horse at the tie rack. He tied Monte beside that horse and was in the act of ducking under the hitch rail when something odd struck him. He straightened and turned to look again at Monte's companion. The horse was a bay with a roached mane and wore a small brand high on its neck, a sort of wiggling line with a circle at the top. That would be, Jim guessed, the old Mexico version of a Picket Pin brand. But it was not the brand that intrigued him. What did take his eye was the saddle on the horse. Jim Barre recognized that saddle. He should have known it, for, during the past two years, he had put his leg across it many a time. The bay horse was carrying the saddle that Waco had sold so blithely back in Carver City. Jim, having made the identification, went on into the store.

Inside the door he stopped in surprise. Stupe Wadell stood at the counter, talking to Thad Gaskin. For an instant Jim paused, and then walked on toward the two men. As he approached, Wadell turned. That Wadell also was surprised was apparent from the expression on his face.

71

"Hello, Barre," he said. "I didn't know you were in this country."

"Waco an' I came down to trap wolves," Jim answered, shaking Wadell's hand. "You're kind of a surprise yourself."

"I got tired of Carver City," Wadell said shortly. "Thought I'd try makin' an honest livin' for a while. I heard that there was a job open down here, an' drifted down to see if I could get it."

Jim nodded. It was on the tip of his tongue to ask Wadell where he had acquired the saddle, but he checked the words. Wadell must be working for Tayler. That would explain the saddle.

"How much do I owe you, Mister Gaskin?" Wadell asked, turning from Jim.

Gaskin added figures scrawled on a piece of paper. "A carton of Duke's Mixture," he said, "papers . . . the whole thing comes to three dollars."

"How do you like your job?" Jim asked as Wadell paid the bill.

"Huh?" Wadell turned. "Oh, the job. I haven't seen about it yet. I'm just headed there."

That was, patently, a lie. If Stupe Wadell had not been hired by Tayler, how had he come by the saddle? Jim held his peace. It was none of his business if Wadell lied, and it was none of his business who had hired Wadell. If the former night deputy didn't want to tell the truth, all right. Anyway, this — to Jim Barre's certain knowledge — was not the first time Stupe Wadell had lied.

"Here's your change," Gaskin said. "You go on south an' take the first road that turns off east. That'll bring you to Tayler's."

"Thanks," Wadell said shortly. "You doin' any good with your trappin', Barre?"

"Pretty fair," Jim answered. "We've got a few pelts."

"I'll maybe try that myself if I don't catch on with an outfit," Wadell declared. "Well, so long." He nodded to Gaskin, raised a hand in salutation to Jim, and strode toward the door. When he was gone, Gaskin made a little movement.

"What can I do for you?" he asked.

Jim still stared at the door. "What does Tayler brand his horses?" he asked abruptly.

"A hatchet on the hip," Gaskin answered. "Did you want somethin', Mister Barre?"

Jim recited his needs absently. He was thinking that Stupe Wadell had certainly left in a hurry. He hadn't stayed around and talked.

Eight

Saddle Search

The front door opened quickly, and Marilee Clark came hurrying back through the store. "Who owns that horse?" she began, and then stopped, seeing Jim. Gaskin put a carton of matches beside the coffee and the baking powder.

"I guess that's my horse," Jim said.

The girl's eyes blazed. "That's my father's saddle!" she announced. "How did you get it?" There was anger in her voice and a tinge also of anxiety.

Gaskin was leaning against the counter now, both his hands hidden below it.

"Your brother left it with me," Jim answered steadily.

"I don't believe you!" the girl flared. "Dale and I looked for that saddle everywhere. I believe you took it. Maybe you killed him for it."

"Now wait a minute," Jim demanded. "You don't . . . ?"

Gaskin's hands came out from beneath the counter. They gripped a shotgun, and the muzzles of the weapon swung to cover Jim Barre.

"You stand still," Gaskin rasped. "Marilee, you skip across to the ranger camp an' get Captain Ringold, if he's there. Run now."

The girl hesitated only an instant, then her heels sounded in a swift tattoo as she ran toward the door.

"Just keep still," Gaskin warned.

Jim Barre kept still.

It seemed a long time before he heard Ringold and Marilee Clark coming. The muzzles of the shotgun were unwavering and no more uncompromising than the face of the man who held the gun. Standing there, Jim Barre had plenty of time to estimate Thad Gaskin, and to check and revise his opinion. The storekeeper, Jim decided, was a tough old jigger who would just as soon shoot a man as look at him. Then Ringold's drawling voice relieved the tension.

"Well, Jim," the ranger drawled, "looks like they've caught up with you. What you holdin' the gun on him for, Gaskin?"

"Tell him, Marilee," Gaskin said.

"I told him." The girl's voice was breathless. Taking his eyes from the shotgun, Jim glanced at Marilee. She had been running, and her hair was disheveled by the wind, and her cheeks were flushed. She was mighty pretty, Jim thought.

"What's all this about a saddle?" Ringold was grinning.

Relief flooded Jim Barre.

"Put down your gun, Thad," the ranger continued. "Jim won't run away."

Slowly Gaskin lowered the shotgun, and Jim Barre turned to confront the ranger and the girl.

"Now what about the saddle?" Ringold said.

"It's my father's saddle," Marilee announced. "I know it is. Ask him how he got it."

"How did you get it, Jim?"

In a few sentences Jim told how he had acquired the saddle. "I didn't feel like makin' a claim on you," he concluded, looking steadily at Marilee Clark, "for what I'd loaned your brother, so I just kept the saddle."

There was a small pause, then Ringold said: "I've known this boy a long time, Miss Clark. I've never known him to lie."

Bright red suffused Marilee's cheeks. She looked swiftly at

Jim Barre and then lowered her eyes. "It was my father's saddle," she said. "I . . . Dale and I had been looking for it and for Chino Joe. We thought . . . well. . . ." She stopped in confusion.

"You're welcome to the saddle," Jim said stiffly. He was angry, both at the treatment he had received and at the fact that he had been placed in a false position. Ringold had vouched for his veracity, but that did not mean that Marilee Clark and Gaskin believed him.

The girl looked up again. "I'm sorry," she said softly. "I believe you, Mister Barre. It was just that seeing that old saddle once more upset me. And Dale was murdered, and. . . ." Tears gathered in her brown eyes, and she turned swiftly away.

"Why, I don't blame you none," Jim said awkwardly. "I should have told you about the saddle in Carver City, but you were upset, an' I didn't want to bother you, an' I thought. . . ." He broke off. He was about to say that he had thought Dale Clark had put over a shabby bargain.

The girl looked at him again. "Did Dale say anything when he left the saddle?" she asked. "Did he say anything about finding it, or about Joe?"

"I wasn't there," Jim answered. "He left the saddle with Waco. But I don't think he said anything. If he did, Waco didn't tell it to me."

"Why did your brother want the saddle?" Ringold asked the girl.

"I told you that," Gaskin answered the question. "This is the saddle that Howie was ridin' when he was killed. Ain't that right, Marilee?"

The girl nodded. "And Chino Joe brought it back to the ranch when he came in," she said. "Dale and I weren't at home. Father had sent us to school in El Paso that year. Joe brought Father's body back, and he told Uncle Thad that Father had said to give the saddle to Dale or me . . . that it was valuable. Joe had reached Father before he died. Then Joe was frightened by all the talk of lynching by people that believed he'd killed Father, and about the mine that Father was supposed to have found, so he ran away, and took the saddle with him. Dale and I have been looking for Joe and the saddle ever since."

The three men exchanged glances. "An' Joe was killed down in a shack on Tayler's ranch," Ringold said slowly. "At least we think it was Joe. We never found a body."

With a start, Jim Barre recalled something he had heard in Carver City. He spoke quickly. "When Dale was killed, Stupe Wadell shot a Mexican that was wearin' Dale's belt. I talked to Bill Murry about that, an' Murry was sore. He said that the Mexican . . . Pancho Vigil was his name . . . had been teamin' around with a half-breed Chinese an' Mexican. Do you suppose it could have been Joe?"

Ringold nodded slowly, and his eyes narrowed. "That was probably Chino Joe," he agreed. "Dale could have found the saddle an' Joe both in Carver City. Maybe Joe went broke an' hocked the saddle, or sold it. But why was Dale killed?"

"An' there's a reason for that, too," Gaskin said dryly. "Howie Clark *did* find a mine across the river. It's wire gold, an' rich. There're men that have been tryin' to find it ever since. If Dale found Chino Joe an' got to talk to him, he might have got a line on the mine. It might be that somebody tried to get it out of Dale, an', when he wouldn't tell, they killed him."

"Dale's hands were tied," Jim said eagerly. "Waco saw that. An' he'd been beat up an' cut. He. . . ." He stopped.

With a little gasp, Marilee had turned from the men and was moving blindly toward the back of the store. In the excitement of the moment the men had been oblivious to the girl's reaction to their conversation.

"I'm a ring-tailed fool," Jim said remorsefully, taking a futile step to follow the girl. "I never thought. . . ."

"None of us did," Gaskin returned. "You stay here." And with that order, he hurried after Marilee, leaving Ringold and Jim Barre looking at each other helplessly.

"Gaskin thinks it was the two Lemoine boys you saw at the camp," Ringold said after a moment. "If Chino had time to get down here from Carver City, so did they." There was significance in the ranger's tone.

"Waco an' me," Jim said slowly, "heard Chino yell in the shack. He was pleadin' with 'em, yellin' that he didn't know, an' beggin' 'em to let him go."

A silence followed. "I reckon I want the Lemoines," Ringold said heavily. "I wanted 'em before this. Now I want 'em bad. Let's get that saddle in here, Jim. Maybe we can find out somethin' from it."

They left the store together.

When the two, Jim Barre and the ranger captain, returned, Jim carrying the saddle, Thad Gaskin and Marilee were beside the counter once more.

"We thought we'd better look at this," Ringold said gruffly. "Have you got a screwdriver, Thad?"

Gaskin turned away and, returning shortly with the desired tool, handed it to Ringold, who attacked the saddle. Using the screwdriver, he loosened the strings that held the skirts and lining together, and spread them apart. There was nothing between skirts and lining. The jockeys were lifted, disclosing nothing. Nor was there anything beneath the seat, in the *tapaderos,* or on the *rosaderos*. Thorough as was the search, it disclosed exactly nothing — no words or marks on the leather, no slip of paper. Ringold tapped the horn of the dismembered saddle with the handle of his screwdriver and looked at Marilee.

"Nothin' here," he said. "Are you sure that this was your daddy's saddle?"

The girl nodded. "I'm sure of it," she said. "I remember the carving on the fenders and the *tapaderos,* and I made those spur tracks across the seat myself. I fell off one time, and my spur rolled across. There used to be silver ornaments on the skirts, and there was a big silver plate on the horn, but they're gone now."

"Likely Chino Joe took them off an' sold 'em," Ringold commented. "They're sure gone. Nothin' but rawhide on the horn."

This was true. The big, pie-plate horn was covered with rawhide, and rawhide was wrapped around its shank and the A of the fork.

"Well," the ranger captain continued, "I've torn the saddle apart. You can put it back together, Jim." He looked at Marilee, his long face kindly. "Reckon it's a washout, girl."

Marilee nodded.

Gaskin placed his arm around her shoulder "Don't feel too bad," he said.

"I . . . I think I'll go home, Uncle Thad." Marilee looked up at the storekeeper.

Jim turned from the work of reassembling the saddle. "I'll leave this here for you," he said. "It was your daddy's. . . ."

"No," interrupted Marilee. "Dale left it with you. I want you to have it. I'm sorry about what I said. I recognized the saddle the minute I saw it, and just for a moment I thought. . . ." She broke off, slipped from beneath Gaskin's arm, and, with no other word, went toward the door. Uncomfortably the men watched her leave.

"She's been countin' on learnin' a lot when she found the

79

saddle," Gaskin said quietly. "She's disappointed. Well . . .
it's tough."

"Tough," Jim echoed. "I'll leave the saddle here for her."

"No. Take it along. She wants you to have it, an' I don't
want it here to remind her of things. I'll get the rest of your
stuff. Coffee, matches, bakin' powder. What else was it you
said?"

"Salt," Jim answered mechanically.

"I'll get it from the storehouse."

Gaskin turned away, and methodically Jim pulled a string
through leather and tied it.

"Sometimes," Ringold rasped, "I wish I could take time
off an' tend to things like this."

Jim nodded glumly, working at another string.

"But I can't," the ranger captain pursued his thoughts.
"I've got other business. If it wasn't for this thing along the
border, I'd start after the Lemoines an' get 'em."

"I'll take that off your hands," Jim said quietly. "They
killed Chino Joe."

Ringold glanced sharply at his companion. "No, you
won't," he said positively. "You'll stay right where you are.
You've got a bigger job than chasin' the Lemoines, an' you
don't know that they killed Chino Joe. You just think they
did. If you work for me, you'll take orders."

Jim turned rebellious eyes toward the speaker. "Maybe I
won't take orders," he said. "I ain't a ranger."

"Look, Jim," Ringold said seriously. "I need you here,
right now. You stay with me in this business, an' I'll promise
you that, as soon as I can, I'll take the whole outfit an' run this
other business down. Will you deal that way?"

For a long minute Jim Barre was silent. Then he nodded
and said slowly: "I'll deal that way, Captain. But I won't
promise what will happen to the Lemoines, if I find them.

80

The way I feel now, if I see 'em, I'll shoot first an' ask questions afterward."

"I don't blame you." Ringold was sympathetic. "An' I'll write to Bill Murry at Carver City an' tell him to keep busy on that end. Bill will do it."

Jim Barre picked up the saddle. He had restrung it and was ready to ride. Gaskin was returning from the warehouse, carrying a small sack of salt, and Ringold, having achieved his point, concluded softly: "She's a mighty fine girl, Jim."

The ranger captain accompanied Jim out of Gaskin's store and stood by, while Jim resaddled Monte and tied on his sack of supplies. There was further talk from the ranger captain while Jim worked.

Ringold was worried. Word had come from Austin that a crisis was approaching in Mexico. There was a rumor of rifles being transported south, and another rumor that Porfirio Díaz had abdicated in Mexico City and was fleeing the country. Troops were stationed at Brownsville. Fort Bliss was sending out patrols, and there were detachments of cavalry at Del Río and Presidio. All this worried the ranger captain.

"I've got men located where I think I need 'em," he told Jim, "but the trouble is that you can't trust a Mexican. They'll bring you word of somethin', an' you go to look into it, an' then somethin' happens while you're gone. Not all of 'em are that way, but they're mighty uncertain. What I want to do is *keep* things from happenin', not catch the man after it happens. An' when they blow up across the river, we'll have our hands full. You keep a sharp lookout, Jim. Maybe you'd better quit trappin' an' just ride the river for a while."

"Waco," Jim answered, "has already made connections down at a *pueblito* below us. He's been droppin' in there . . . an' we've been watchin' the trails that come up from the river.

I think we'll do all right where we are for a while."

"You get around an' talk to people," Ringold ordered. "Talk to these Mexicans an' learn what you can. You haven't run across anythin' yet?"

"Nothin' for certain," Jim answered. "You'll know as soon as we do."

"All right," Ringold returned. "Just stay the way you are for a while, then. But don't let this other business sidetrack you. You keep your eyes an' your ears open, an' tell me what you learn."

He was through with his saddling then and ready to go. Ringold shook hands with him. "Don't forget," the captain warned. "Don't go back on me now, you an' Ibolt."

"We won't forget," Jim assured. "An' we won't go back on you."

The afternoon was waning as Jim Barre, the flour sack containing his purchases bumping against his leg, rode back toward the camp and Waco. There were many things to occupy his mind as he rode south. First was the warning that Ringold had given him. Jim Barre, from past experience, knew how the Texas Rangers worked. They moved into a country where there was trouble, and that trouble was cleaned up. But this time Ringold was there to prevent trouble, and so he needed spies. The way to do that was to make a great many acquaintances and friends, particularly among the natives — make them believe in you. Then a word here, a hint dropped there, a rumor heard and followed out, and a man had information to report.

But that sort of thing took time, and, too, a man had to have a good reason to be in a country, or else he aroused suspicion. The way to get the necessary extra time was to run fewer traps. That was easy. But a wolfer that didn't trap would be an object of conjecture and suspicion. Waco and

Jim were already established as wolfers, and, if they changed their occupation, it would not look good.

Jim Barre had no illusions. He knew the way news and rumor flashed across a country that was almost unpopulated. It was odd, but he would bet that in the ranch houses, in the little native settlements, in the solitary camps all along this section of the border, the word had already been passed that there was a ranger company at Gaskin's Crossroads, that there were two strangers trying to trap wolves on Tayler's range, and that there had been a fight and a killing in a deserted cow camp close to where the wolfers trapped.

Putting this line of thought aside, Jim considered other matters. The reasoning that Ringold and Gaskin and he had followed when they talked about the murder of Dale Clark, the search of the saddle, all those facts and conjectures were dissected, one by one. Jim was not satisfied concerning the saddle. The half-breed, Chino Joe, had held onto it for two years, and surely there must be something about the old hull that was valuable. Still Ringold hadn't found it.

And why had the saddle been for sale back in Carver City? Had Joe gone broke and hocked it? What was the cause? Thoughts of the saddle he bestrode brought to Jim Barre's mind the recollection of that other saddle. With surprise he recalled that he had not mentioned it to Ringold, had not told the ranger captain about Stupe Wadell and Tayler, and the bargain Waco had made with the ranchman. Then he shrugged. Certainly there had been no call for his telling Ringold about that. It did not fit into this other picture. But still, there was a fact that stood out like a pine tree on a bald knob — Stupe Wadell had been lying when he said that he hadn't got a job yet. Stupe had bought a carton of tobacco, and a man traveling through a country generally bought his tobacco by the sack. Besides, if Stupe hadn't hired out to

Tayler, what was he doing riding Jim Barre's old saddle?

The trail that led to camp branched off the road here, and Jim turned Monte toward it. He hurried now, for dusk was approaching. Monte, knowing that he was homeward bound where he would get rid of his load, hurried along, trotting over the trail. Jim thrust the maze of thoughts back in his mind, shelving them. He would thresh the whole thing out with Waco after he reached camp. And when Waco heard the story, he would probably arrive at the same conclusion that Jim Barre had reached — that the Lemoines might be connected with the killing of Dale Clark, just as they were implicated in the murder of Chino Joe.

But there was someone with the Lemoines. There had been four horses along the corral fence at the old cow camp, and Jim had glimpsed someone inside the door when the sudden battle began. Surely there had been others with the Lemoines in the camp the night that Chino Joe had died. The whole thing, Jim told himself savagely, revolved about a gold mine — a fabulous lost mine that Marilee's father, old Howie Clark, was supposed to have discovered. Dale Clark, searching for a clue to that mine, was dead, murdered. Chino Joe, perhaps possessing a clue, was also dead. And there were living men who would kill again, just on the chance of getting track of that mine, when possibly there was no mine at all. Gold and the things men would do for it!

Between the ridge top and the camp, the ground was fairly clear of brush. Dusk had come, and down below him Jim could see the dark bulk of camp and corral. Presently the moon would rise, and all the little valley would be flooded with silver, but now it lay in shadow, and, amidst the shadow, a spot of light glowed. Waco had the door open, and the firelight cast a welcome glow. Lifting his voice, Jim called: "Hiyah . . . Waco!"

There was no answer. Briefly the spot of light was blotted out, and then showed again as someone crossed the door. Waco, Jim thought, must be sore because his partner had stayed away so long. Well, he'd get over that when Jim told him what he knew.

Jim stopped Monte beside the corral, swung down, and reached up for the saddle strings that held the sack. As he raised the knot, Monte, frightened, shied suddenly, and as he moved, a blow from the darkness grazed Jim's hat, knocking it off, and striking against his shoulder.

Momentarily confused by the swiftness of the unexpected attack, Jim went down, rolling on his side, his shoulder numb. As he rolled, he heard Waco's voice, a high squall: "Look out, Jim! They're. . . ."

The voice broke off. Above Jim Barre flame ringed the muzzle of a gun, gravel spurted into his face, stinging against his cheek, and a shot crashed, almost deafening him with its nearness.

Reaction was instinctive — no process of thought was connected with Jim's swift response. Even as he completed his roll, coming over on his back, his gun was out and cocked. Twice he shot, squarely up into the dark blotch above him. He heard his attacker crash back into the dried ocotillo stems of the corral. Then Jim came up, almost bouncing to his feet, the numbness gone from his shoulder, and his gun cocked and ready for another shot. There was no movement beside the ocotillo fence, and, whirling, Jim ran toward the lighted door of the camp.

Before he reached it, the light was blotted out once again. Jim, firing as he ran, sent a swift shot toward the opening and was answered. He checked, dropping down to take cover, and fired again in answer to the shot, sending his lead searching into the darkness where he had seen the gunflame. One more shot in his Colt.

Then from the shack Waco yelled: "They're outside, Jim. Outside! Three of 'em!"

Nine

Waco's Story

In spite of his own danger, Jim felt relief well up in him at the sound of Waco's voice. The little man could still yell, though something prevented his taking an active part in the battle. Hammer at half cock, Jim slid spent shells from his Colt and stuffed in fresh loads fumbled from his belt. Six shots in the Colt. No use carrying an empty chamber now.

There was sudden movement to the left of the shack. Jim centered a shot on the spot, heard a man yelp — not from hurt, but fright, he thought — and he scuttled to his right, changing position. Hang it! He surely wished that Waco could have a chunk of this.

Somewhere over beside the shack, a man began to shout: "Carl! Carl! Are you all right, Carl?"

There was no answer to the call. Carl, Jim thought grimly, must be the lad beside the ocotillo fence. Anyhow, Carl was not doing any yelling in reply to the call. Jim moved again, more cautiously than ever, circling to come above the shack. As he moved, he heard a sound, paused, turning toward it, gun lifted, and then there was a rattle of stones and the rasp of a horse's hoofs as the animal broke from stand to full run. Jim fired twice at the horseman that flashed across the light from the door, aimed again, and checked his finger on the trigger. The rider was gone, crashing into the brush that lay to the south of the camp.

The man who had called for Carl lifted his voice again in anger: "Blast you, Agapito!"

Waco had yelled that there were three of them. One was

87

down, over by the corral. One had taken a horse and pulled his freight. That left one more. Jim Barre resumed his cautious circling. The remaining attacker was behind the shack, and to the east the edge of the rising moon showed above the ridge. Jim hastened. He wanted to gain his vantage point before the moon came up. Then, with moonlight, he would make it mighty tough on that jasper. He'd learn that boy to suck eggs.

Evidently the man behind the shack had the same idea as Jim's, but in reverse. There was a minute of silence, during which time Jim moved about ten long yards. Then, again, there was the sudden rattle and clatter of a moving horse. Jim straightened up and swore. The shack was between himself and the horse. He had come too far. And this last rider was making tracks toward the east, making them mighty fast.

Half the moon was over the ridge now, and there was light on the opposite slope. Gun ready, Jim reached the dark side of the camp and slid along the wall.

"Waco," he said, low voiced.

Wrathfully his partner answered. "Come in here, dang it! Let me loose!"

Still cautious, Jim Barre slid along the side of the shack, reached the door, and looked around the edge. Waco, hands and feet tied, lay prone in front of the fireplace. Jim stepped in through the door, slammed it shut, and went hastily to his partner.

The butcher knife from the table sliced through the softly braided pigging strings that bound Waco's wrists and ankles. Righted, the little man sat on the bench while Jim washed a gash on his head, cut away hair, and exposed the ragged lips of the wound. And while his partner worked, Waco talked.

"A dog-gone Mexican!" he raged. "He came in here about two hours after you'd left. Rode in just as pert as you please. I was fleshin' a hide, an' he got off his horse an' come over to watch. Friendly as all get out. We talked along, an' I was pumpin' him, an' all of the time it was Agapito de Griego. First thing I knew, he'd throwed down on me.

"'Manos alta, señor,' he says. Jumpin' Jehoshaphat! I'd left my gun belt on the table. There wasn't nothin' for me to do but put my hands up."

Jim, delving into a pack box, brought out the bottle of horse liniment and uncorked it. Waco, seeing what was about to happen, broke off his tirade to protest: "Don't put that stuff on me, Jim. It burns like blazes."

"Got to stop the bleedin'," Jim countered, and advanced with the bottle.

"My gentle Nellie!" Waco swore, as the liniment bit and burned.

"An' then what happened?" Jim demanded

"Then them two Lemoines come trailin' in," Waco continued. "They was supposed to meet de Griego at that other camp, from what they said, an' they was pretty sore. Them Lemoines are tough. They was all for beefin' me, but de Griego wouldn't have it. They jabbered a while, an' then tied me up. The Lemoines are runnin' guns, Jim. That's what they met de Griego about. He's got a camp on the other side of the Río, an' he come over to fix it up about a shipment. They talked about that, an' then one of the Lemoines kicked me an' asked me where you was. I told him to go to the devil. They talked a while where I couldn't hear 'em, an' then one of 'em come back an' kicked me again.

"'We'll wait for that pardner of yours,' he says. 'We want his saddle.' About that time de Griego come in again. I didn't know how the hell I was goin' to warn you. What happened outside?"

"I came down the trail an' had reached the corral, when

89

somebody jumped me," Jim answered. "Luckily, Monte shied an' made the feller miss. He knocked me down, all right. Then I heard you yell, an' went to work."

Jim was finished with his bandaging by now, and Waco's head was swathed in a white turban.

"Have any luck?" the little man demanded, his eyes keen on Jim's face.

"I think so," his partner answered quietly. "Let's go see. They hit you when you yelled, didn't they?"

"One of them Lemoines did," Waco answered, rising. "Hang it! I'm sore an' raw. De Griego lit a shuck out the door. Then Lemoine followed him, an' I heard the shootin'. Two of 'em left, didn't they?"

"Two," Jim agreed. "Take it easy, Waco. They might still be around."

"Not them." Waco pulled open the door, and they stepped out quickly.

Outside the shack they stopped, listening and searching the yard with keen eyes. The moon had silvered the hollow now, and the shadows of the minor growth were long and treacherous, affording concealment.

For perhaps five minutes the partners stood there, and then Jim stepped forward. "Gone for keeps," he said tersely, and led the way toward the corral.

Against the ocotillo fence a man lay sprawled, sightless eyes lifted to the moonlit sky.

"Lemoine," Jim said slowly. "The other one hollered for Carl, so this must be him."

"He's awful dead," Waco said, rising from his examination. "This is the one that took my rifle."

"It's there against the fence," Jim announced.

The Krag was leaning against the fence, looking almost like a misplaced branch of ocotillo.

"You done a thorough job on him," the little man commented, picking up the gun.

"Monte, shyin' the way he did, was lucky," Jim said. "These fellows are the devil on clubbin' a gun, Waco. That's what they used on Chino Joe, an' that's what they used on us."

"They'll get a few more lessons, an' we'll learn 'em that a gun's to shoot with," Waco promised grimly. "That is, if they live. This 'un will never learn nothin' any more."

"There's Monte up on the slope with Oscar an' the mule," Jim drawled. "I'll get him an' unsaddle. He just about saved my life."

Waco slid the bolt of the Krag back and forth, and clicked the safety. "I'll go along with you," he announced. "You stayed a mighty long time at the Crossroads, Jim."

"Had a lot of things happen myself," Jim informed him. They walked side by side, away from the corral to where the horses stood on the moonlit slope. "I'll tell you why by an' by. Right now, I've got an idea."

"An idea?"

"Yeah." Jim's voice was thoughtful. "This Agapito de Griego came over here to talk about gettin' some guns from the Lemoines. That's what you said, isn't it?"

"Yeah." There was no comprehension in Waco's tone.

"Ringold," Jim continued slowly, "is mighty anxious about guns an' such. An' we promised to help him out."

"So?" Waco said.

"So you heard de Griego say that he had a bunch of his men on the other side of the creek." Jim spoke firmly now. "I think I'll try to slip over there an' scout 'em. Mebbe we can't tell Ringold where the guns are comin' from, but I might learn where they're goin'."

There followed a little silence. The men had stopped, and

the horses and the mule, ears pointed, were looking at them.

"It ain't ever a smart idea for a man to get killed," Waco said reflectively, "but, then, he can't hope to live for always. I'll just go with you."

Ten

Night Scouting

Jim did not want the smaller man to go along on this expedition, but Waco was adamant, and short of tying him again there was no way to dodge his company. Jim waited while his partner saddled and put the Krag in his saddle boot, and then, side by side, they rode across the clearing and toward the river.

"De Griego helped himself to my six-shooter," Waco announced when they were halfway to the southern boundary of the clearing. "So I just took Lemoine's." Glancing at his companion, Jim could see the heavy belt sagging about the little man's waist. "An' I'm goin' to have to put galluses on it to keep it from comin' down around my knees," Waco concluded. "Lemoine must have been a couple of yards around the middle."

They reached the brush then and entered the trail that led down to the river. Jim made no comment. Now was not the time to talk. Now was the time to peer through the moonlight, to examine every shadow, every rock, every brush clump.

Monte walked slowly. The horse was tired. They were, Jim thought idly, going to have to do something about their horses. Both Monte and Oscar were getting too much riding. Waco, a trifle in the lead, stopped the grulla suddenly.

"Here we are," he said in a low voice. "Better scout it on foot, hadn't we?"

Silently both men dismounted and tied their horses. Waco slid the Krag from its scabbard, and Jim lifted his own short-barreled, lever-action Winchester from its sheath.

When he turned, Waco had removed the too large cartridge belt and was stuffing the Colt into his waist overalls. That finished, the little man slipped out shells from the belt loops and hung belt and scabbard on his saddle horn.

They were almost at the brink of the river cañon. Rocks and brush were all about, and immediately before them was the sheer break of the cañon, a crevasse cutting into it. Through that crevasse the trail led, and Jim, stepping forward, looked down.

"We'll take it afoot," he said. "Then, if it looks all right, one of us can come back an' get the horses."

Waco nodded. De Griego, fleeing, had made this sheer descent on horseback, and neither Jim Barre nor Waco would have quibbled over doing the same thing under ordinary circumstances. But these conditions were not ordinary. The two men were not familiar with the trail, the moonlight was treacherous, and somewhere down that path Agapito de Griego, or one of his men, might well be waiting. Again, the purpose of the two companions was to descend silently and undetected. They could best do that on foot.

Having made his decision, Jim stepped forward. Waco, his hat sitting rakishly atop his bandaged head, waited for an instant, and then followed.

They found the trail good — plenty good for a horse. It was narrow, and twisted back and forth, but the slope was not so steep as it appeared from above. Once a rock rolled from beneath Waco's foot and went slithering down, and the two men stopped, waiting until the noise died away and the cañon was quiet again.

"It's good enough," Jim said, keeping his voice low. "We'll go back for the horses."

"Wait!" Waco said tensely. "Somethin' down there on the bench, see? In the shadow?"

94

Jim peered down to where the trail came out on a little bench. He could see nothing unusual, but, if Waco had detected motion or something out of place, it was well to stop.

"See?" Waco slid down and joined his partner. "There by the big rock?"

"I don't see a thing," Jim said truthfully.

"Somethin' moved." Waco was past Jim now, and staring toward the bench. "Might have been a rabbit. Might be 'most anythin'. I'll slide on down an' see."

Before Jim could restrain him, Waco was gone, moving down the trail. The bench was not fifteen feet below them.

Emerging from shadow, Waco started across the bench toward the big rock he had indicated, and from the darkness across the cañon a flame bloomed and then came the crash and roar of an explosion, beating back and forth between the cañon walls. Waco was lost to view in the shadow of the rock, and Jim, hearing the high whine of a ricocheting bullet, made the last fifteen feet of the trail to the bench in one, swift, headlong rush. Once again the gun from across the cañon roared, as Jim dived for the shadow of the rock, Winchester across his chest, his thumb on the hammer. As he dropped down into the shelter, he heard Waco cursing.

"Blacker than midnight in a cellar," the little man snarled. "Here we are, right out on the bench an' them in the dark. They caught us just like we was kids in a pantry."

To some extent he was right. The opposite side of the cañon was shadowed, the moon not yet having risen high enough to light it. And, too, Jim and Waco were marooned, but, sheltered by their rock fort, they were in no serious trouble. Moonlight makes uncertain shooting, and a man in shadow cannot pull his front sight down into the notch of the rear with any sureness. Jim grunted and then laughed lightly.

"We got too ambitious," he said. "Looks like we're here for a spell."

"Till the moon goes down," Waco concurred. "No use of takin' a chance gettin' back up the trail, an' I sure ain't goin' to try to go down it."

"Nor me," said Jim.

Neither man was afraid, but they did not intend to be any more foolhardy than they had been already. If the matter had been important, they would, despite the rifles across the cañon, have made a break from their shelter. But there was no use in taking a chance on getting shot simply because they wanted to explore. Waco lay at the end of the rock, concealed by its shadow, and peered off across the cañon and the river.

"They got to shoot three hundred yards, anyhow," he computed the distance. "They couldn't hit us at that range, if they had daylight to shoot by. I think there's some of them right at the bottom of the trail, Jim. Maybe they'll try to come up an' get us."

"Maybe," Jim agreed. "An' then, mebbe not."

There was a brief interlude, then a match flamed in Waco's cupped hands, and Jim could smell the smoke of his cigarette.

"We'd ought to've scouted the bottom of the cañon," Waco announced. "We don't know where the crossin's are for sure."

"We know there's one below some place, an' we know there's one at Pajaritos," Jim answered.

"That's so," Waco said thoughtfully. "An' that other camp . . . the one where the half-breed was killed . . . is the place they're usin' on the Texas side. We know that."

Jim did not answer his partner. A good many things that had been partially veiled were exposed now.

"What happened at the Crossroads?" Waco asked suddenly.

"Several things," answered Jim. He was at the other end of the big rock, scanning the dark side of the cañon, seeing nothing, but using his eyes as best he could, and listening, too, for the telltale clink of metal on rock or other sound that would tell of the trail's being used.

As Jim watched, he recounted the occurrences of the day, his speech broken by long pauses when both men listened.

"Wadell's hooked up with Tayler," Waco said when Jim had completed his tale. "That's how come he was ridin' your old saddle."

"That's what I thought," Jim agreed.

"Wadell ain't too good a man, Jim," Waco said. "He's got a bad reputation, an' he worked pretty hard to get it." After a moment's pause he mused: "An' you never found a thing in that old saddle. Dale Clark bought it because he thought he'd learn somethin' from it. Funny. You an' me both thought that Clark was puttin' somethin' over on you when he borrowed money, an' then left that old saddle for security. An' all the time he was really leavin' a thing he thought was valuable."

"Yeah," Jim agreed. Then: "You know, Waco, I've kind of got that figured out now. Dale must've seen the saddle in the window when we came to town after we'd penned the calves. The stores were all closed, remember? He couldn't get it that night. An' he needed money for somethin'. He sent a telegram to his sister the night we got into town. An' you remember that Bill Murry said that a half-breed Chinaman an' Mexican had been hangin' around Carver City. That must've been Chino Joe. Dale must have seen Chino an' learned somethin' from him. Chino had plenty of time to leave Carver City an' get down here before we did. That's what he did, an' he got killed for doin' it. Likely he was to meet Dale down here. Then Dale got himself killed. . . ."

"Got tortured an' killed," Waco corrected. "His hands were tied, an' he'd been all beat up."

"Wadell an' Murry said his hands weren't tied."

Waco snorted. "I seen it," he said impatiently. "They were tied behind him. You think I can't see?"

"But. . . ." Jim's words were drowned in a crash of concentrated fire from across the cañon, a roar as of six or seven rifles discharged simultaneously. Lead cut into the trail above the bench, sending rocks spurting, a bullet or two whining away as they ricocheted.

"Now what made 'em do that?" Waco demanded petulantly.

"Thought they saw somethin' on the trail," Jim answered. "It's gettin' light across there, Waco."

"When it gets light enough, I'll make some of 'em slide around a little," Waco vowed. "This Krag is built for this kind of shootin'. Two or three hundred yards ain't nothin' for a Krag."

"Anyhow," Jim reverted to his former subject, "it's that blamed gold mine that's doin' the damage. Howie Clark was supposed to have found a mine, an' Chino Joe was supposed to know where it was. The Lemoines, an' whoever else is with 'em, killed Dale on account of that. An' they killed the halfbreed. That's two murders."

"An' mebbe there's another one," drawled Waco. "Mebbe that Mexican, Pancho Vigil, was killed for the same reason."

"You kind of figure that way, too, do you?" Jim asked. "I didn't say it, but Stupe Wadell was sure handy with his second shot that day. Murry didn't like it."

"An' Stupe had a chance to cut Dale's hands free," Waco said. "Look, Jim. Ain't that somethin' beside the cedar across

98

there? See the little cedar right by that bunch of trees? Kind of standin' off by itself? Ain't there somethin' movin' there?"

"It might be," Jim agreed, peering over his shelter. "Maybe it is, Waco."

"Well, then, watch!" Waco ordered.

Jim, concentrating on the spot Waco had indicated, heard his companion move, and the snick of a safety being changed. Then the Krag carbine bellowed, and, across the cañon, rock shattered a good five feet from the place Waco had spotted.

The shot was answered by the rifles across the cañon. One sharp volley blasting the echoes over the river. Waco slid up toward the top of the rock again.

"Where'd I hit?" he demanded.

"About five feet to the left," Jim answered. "You were a way off, Waco. Nobody can shoot good by moonlight."

"My sights are off," Waco said irascibly. "That buzzard that took my rifle got the sights out of line." He slipped the rifle forward, and Jim could see his hand hovering over the leaf sight.

"You can't sight-in a rifle by moonlight!" Jim told him. "Save your shells. That's the trouble with a gun like that . . . there's somethin' always goin' wrong with it. I'll take a Thirty-Thirty every time."

Waco slid down the slope of the rock again. What Jim had said was true. He must wait for daylight to sight his weapon.

"They're sure anxious to keep us here," Waco muttered.

"An' I wonder why," drawled Jim. "I'll bet you that they're keepin' us located while they're up to somethin' some place else."

"Likely," Waco grunted. "Anyhow, we can't do much about it."

"We're goin' to have to report Lemoine's death to Captain Ringold," Jim stated. "An' we're goin' to have to do somethin' about our horses. They're ridden down right now."

A silence fell between the partners. Then Waco said: "They aren't comin' across, Jim, an' they ain't goin' to try to get us. They just want us to stay right here, an' I reckon we'll oblige 'em. Why don't you stretch out an' rest a while? I'll keep a lookout."

Waco's observations seemed reasonable, and Jim was bone weary. He shifted position, turning on his back.

"Then I'll spell you," he said. "When it gets dark, we'll go up on top again."

Waco grunted, and quiet fell over the bench and all along the cañon.

Jim was wakened from a doze by Waco's voice. "Moon's about down, Jim."

The big man stretched, sat up, and looked at the sky. There was still moonlight on the land above, but the cañon was in shadow. Waco was beside him.

"Might as well go," Jim said.

They left the shelter of the rock, moving cautiously back across the bench. There were no sounds other than those they themselves made, no alarm, no shots from beyond the river.

"Probably could've left an hour ago," Waco grumbled. "No use of takin' chances, though."

At the top of the trail they found the horses waiting patiently. Mounting, riding through the dying moonlight, they went back toward the camp. Before they reached the little clearing, they circled and then, fairly sure that there were no unwelcome visitors about, rode boldly in. The night air was chilly, and both men were stiff. After turning the horses out, they went into the little *jacal* where some warmth from the dead fire lingered.

"An' no rest for the wicked," Waco drawled, when Jim had barred the door and closed and barred the crude shutter of the window. "I'd like to sleep a week someday, Jim, but I reckon today ain't the day."

He stretched out on his bed, not even bothering to remove his boots, and Jim Barre, likewise lying down, looked through the darkness toward his partner. What a good little man Waco was!

In the morning they were up early, moving about the camp, making ready for the day's work. Within half an hour they were ready to attack the business before them. The camp lay deserted. Nothing happened as they scouted the clearing, each taking a segment of the circle. Joining again, they walked together to the slope where the mule, with Oscar and Monte, grazed.

"An' there's no rest for you, neither," Waco said, spreading his loop and putting it over his horse's wise head. "Come on. I'll take your hobbles off, Oscar."

"Why do you call him Oscar?" Jim asked curiously, bending to remove Monte's hobbles. "Any reason?"

"Oscar's one of them old Mexican grullas," Waco explained. "When he's got good grass to work on, he grows a regular mustache. I used to know a Swede named Oscar that had a mustache an' pretty near as much hair in his ears as the grulla's got. So I just called the horse Oscar."

The mule followed the horses into the camp. There Waco caught her, and saddles were placed on all the animals. Under ocotillo stems lay the tarp-covered body of Carl Lemoine. Working together silently, the two men loaded the body on the mule. Then, returning to the horses, they mounted and struck north along the trail.

The ranger camp at Gaskin's Crossroads was a scene of

activity when Jim and Waco arrived. Ringold, coming out to meet them, listened to their story with an expressionless face, nodding from time to time as a point was made.

"Lemoine'll have to be buried," he said, when the tale was finished. "An' I'll have to have Gaskin look at him. Gaskin's a J. P. I'll tend to that."

Jim nodded. Ringold was dispensing with the formalities that usually accompanied the killing of a man. As a ranger captain, operating in the field, he could eliminate certain processes of the law.

"An' I'll have to make a report to Austin," the ranger officer continued. "We're movin' camp down to Tayler's place. It's handy, an' we can get horses when we need them. Jim, I think you an' your pardner better come along with us."

"Why, Captain?"

Ringold frowned. "They're after you," he said. "They're after that saddle. An' there's a Lemoine left, not to speak of Agapito. I'd be a heap better pleased if you were with me."

Waco bristled. "We can look after ourselves," he declared. "We ain't babies."

Ringold grinned. "I know that," he agreed. "Just the same, I'd like to have you where I can keep an eye on you. Too many things happen to you two when you're alone. You tie up with us at the Hatchet Ranch." There was a finality in the officer's voice that brooked no objection. Still Waco demurred.

"We got traps out, an' we got an outfit," he said.

Ringold nodded. "You can pick that stuff up an' join me at Tayler's," he said curtly. "You could do that today. You know where the Hatchet is, don't you? It's about six miles above the town on Pajaritos Creek."

"Dang it," Waco growled. "We're trappin', an' we're doin' pretty good. We. . . ."

"I'll look for you at Tayler's tonight," Ringold interrupted. "I'll have another job for you, but right now I'd feel a lot better, if you were with me." He turned abruptly and walked away, calling for his sergeant.

Eleven

Rangers Ride

Waco stared rebelliously at the captain's broad back. When Ringold was out of earshot, he spoke. "Where's he get off, givin' us orders? We ain't rangers, are we?"

Jim shook his head. He knew that, eventually, they would do as Ringold had requested, but in the meantime Waco had to let off steam.

"We promised to help him," Jim said mildly.

"Then we'd better tell him we've done our helpin'," Waco retorted.

Again Jim shook his head. "I made a deal with Ringold," he said. "I told him we'd help him out, an' he promised that, as soon as he could, he'd take his whole outfit an' work on Dale Clark's murder."

Waco snorted, still rebellious. "We got our traps all set an' our camp made, an' he tells us to pull up an' join him, just like that. What's he think we are? Kids?"

"We'll go back to trappin', if you want to, Waco," Jim said quietly. "I'll go tell Ringold that we won't hook up with him, an' we'll go on back. Of course, he said that he had a job for us. . . ." He let the sentence die unfinished.

Waco kicked a boot heel into the ground. "Oh, all right!" he growled petulantly. "We'll go get our stuff an' pick up the traps an' join him then. He's makin' such a point of it." The little man turned toward his horse. "I'll lead the mule," he concluded.

Jim smiled quietly, hiding his amusement from Waco. The little man might paw and bellow, but he was just as curious as

Jim concerning the job that Ringold had in mind.

They did not speak to the ranger captain again before leaving. Ringold was busy. He had sent a man to draft labor from the Crossroads settlement, and two natives, carrying shovels, were already walking toward the camp.

Mounting, the two partners rode away from the busy camp site, past the store and Gaskin's house, and on past the native settlement. Just before they reached the brush to the south of the Crossroads, Jim spoke.

"We'd better angle off an' start from the west end," he suggested. "That way we can pick up that line of traps, get our stuff from the camp, then take up your traps an' hit right on to Tayler's."

Waco nodded silent agreement.

"And we can ride past Pajaritos an' see if anythin' went on there last night," Jim amplified. "That'll be the best idea, don't you think, Waco?"

"We'll have to get right along if we're goin' to make Tayler's tonight," Waco said. "Better shake it up, Jim. If we don't get to camp tonight, papa'll spank!"

Jim made no answer, but increased the pace of his horse. Waco would simmer down if given time. And Waco was right. There was a good big job ahead of them.

Angling west from the Crossroads, not trying to follow any trail, but striking across country, they reached the end of Jim's line of traps just at noon. They followed down that line, lifting the traps and putting them on the pack saddle of the mule. At about two o'clock they reached their camp, and there Waco frankly rebelled.

"I'm goin' to eat here if we never get to Tayler's," he said. "Danged, if I'll go all day an' all night without eatin'. An' danged, if I'm goin' to keep puttin' myself out because of some fool ranger captain. We got to get our stuff together an' pack it anyhow. I'll fix us a bite while you do that, Jim."

Without speaking, Jim set about gathering their supplies and packing them while Waco busied himself at the fireplace. By the time Jim had the bedrolls and equipment gathered up, Waco had cooked a meal.

The two ate the food in silence and set about packing and loading the mule.

"That's that," Waco pronounced as he put the finishing touches to the pack. "Now we'll hang the rest of the traps on when we pick 'em up an' come in to Tayler's, soundin' like a travelin' hardware store. Let's go, Jim."

Jim went to his horse, but Waco, beside his mount, stopped and reached up his hand, pulling the Krag from his saddle boot.

"Now what?" Jim demanded.

"I just remembered that my sights are off," Waco answered. "I'm goin' to target my rifle."

Carrying the Krag, he walked back to the side of the shack and sat down. There was no use in arguing with him. Still ruffled by Ringold's brusqueness, the little man could be obstinate as a mule.

"All right," Jim agreed. "Target her, then."

"You watch," ordered Waco. "That white rock on the hill is just about two hundred yards off. I paced it one day. Now watch where I hit."

He fired, both elbows resting on his crossed legs. Dust flew up. "Low an' about three feet left," Jim announced. Waco worked at the sight. "Again!" he ordered, and once more the Krag bellowed.

"Still low an' left."

Once more Waco fingered the sight, growling under his breath. "Now," he said.

This time, when he fired, the white rock jumped violently.

"Right on," Jim announced.

"Good enough, I guess," Waco announced, thumbing long, blunt-tipped shells into the box magazine of the rifle. "That ought to hold her."

Jim glanced up at the sky. The sun was already working toward the west. There were some miles to ride, and here they were killing time with the Krag. As he looked, he witnessed a minor tragedy. Along the river a bird flew — small, frantic, swift — fleeing for its life. Behind the smaller bird came another, an eagle, wings beating as the bird gained altitude for a final sweep.

"Look!" Jim called.

Both men watched the chase in silence. The eagle, gaining position, closed its wings and came down, a feathered thunderbolt armed with six-inch talons. There was no escape for the smaller quarry. Struck in mid-air, the little bird crumpled and fell, only to be caught and grappled before it could strike the ground. Carrying its prey, the eagle swooped up, and then, sailing, lighted on the top of the ridge east of the camp, a full four hundred yards away.

"The damned murderer," Waco snarled. "You will, will you?" Once more he was cuddling the butt of the Krag against his shoulder, the leaf sight raised.

"You can't hit him," Jim said. "It's too far. . . ."

"Watch!" Waco ordered. The Krag settled into place, became still, steady as a rock, and then Waco's shoulder jerked back under the recoil as the gun spoke. Over on the ridge the eagle flapped, and then dropped from sight, and Waco stood up, grinning at his friend.

"Can't hit him, huh?" the little man chortled. "Try that with your Thirty-Thirty some day!"

"I'm goin' to pace that shot," Jim announced. "You bring the horses, Waco."

Grinning, Waco obeyed, while Jim, starting from the wall of the camp, paced steadily toward the top of the ridge.

When they reached the eagle and stopped, Jim looked up at Waco. "Three hundred and forty paces," he said, a little awe in his voice. "That was a considerable shot, Waco."

Dismounting, the little man went to the eagle and lifted the bird by one great wing, the other pinion dragging on the ground. The heavy slug from the Krag had struck low and gutted the bird.

"Look at them claws," Waco ordered. "How'd you like to have them diggin' into you?"

"Let's see what he killed," Jim said, and stooped to pick up the eagle's victim. "Why, it's a pigeon!" He held the small bird in his hand and examined it curiously. "Pretty near cut the pigeon's head off when he hit it," he said. "What's this here on its leg?"

Waco dropped the eagle and came over to look at the pigeon. "Paper," he announced. "Tied on with thread. Now what . . . ?"

"A carrier pigeon," Jim cut in, fumbling for his pocketknife. He opened the knife and snipped the thread that held the little roll of paper to the bird's thin shank. Dropping the pigeon, he unrolled the paper, while Waco pressed against him, looking over his arm.

"Spanish," Waco said, and then translated: "'Tonight at Pajaritos. Bring eight cases. I have the money.' What's that scrawl at the end, Jim?"

"It looks like de Griego to me," Jim said slowly. "Waco, this has got to get to Ringold, an' right now, too."

Waco nodded and looked expectantly at his partner, waiting for orders. A frown creased Jim's forehead as he studied the slip of paper in his hand. Finally he spoke.

"That's why all the pigeons are at Sanchez's place in

Pajaritos. He's the one on this side. Waco, you ride for there. Get some place above the settlement, so you can watch, but don't let them see you. I'll head straight for Tayler's an' take the mule with me. Ringold said it was on the creek north of Pajaritos. We'll meet you on the creek north of town. Got it?"

"I've got it," Waco assured him. "I'll be there."

Nothing more was necessary. They mounted and rode away, each going his separate way — Jim Barre, leading the mule, striking a direct line for the northeast, Waco angling farther toward the south. Neither man looked back at the little clearing in the brush.

Riding steadily, Jim soon lost sight of his partner. The country climbed toward the Chisos, while the river dropped away. Waco was following the river and Barre the higher country. Jim had gone a mile from the camp when he stopped. To his left, not over a hundred yards away, stood a riderless pinto horse. Noting the absence of a rider in the vicinity, Jim went to investigate.

There was no sign that anyone was near the pinto. One bridle rein had been broken off short at the bit. The other rein was longer, but it, too, was broken. The blanket had worked out from under the saddle and was gone. It needed no great insight for Barre to know that this horse was astray. The pinto, he surmised, had belonged to Carl Lemoine and had run from the camp when Lemoine was killed. Jim rode close, taking down his rope as he approached. The horse was gentle, and Jim caught it without trouble, simply riding up and easing his noose over the pinto's bay-and-white neck. A cursory inspection showed no brand. Jim eased his rope up back of the pinto's ears, took a half hitch around the horse's nose, and rode back to pick up the mule, the pinto following willingly enough.

An hour and a half of steady walk, trot, walk, and lope

brought Jim to the creek that ran southeast toward the river. Smoke showed to his left, and he turned in that direction, topped a rise, and shortly was riding down toward the collection of buildings, corrals, and sheds that was Tayler's Hatchet Ranch. As he approached, Ringold and Tayler came out to meet him.

"Where's Ibolt?" the ranger captain demanded.

"Down below," Jim answered, and then, with a glance at Tayler: "I've got a report, Captain."

"I'll ride on back," Tayler said, and, after staring curiously at Jim Barre and his two lead animals, rode on ahead.

Ringold, falling into place beside Barre, said: "What is it, Jim?"

"This," Jim answered, and passed over the small slip of paper.

The ranger captain read it through and then looked questioningly at his companion. Jim made a succinct report on how the note had come into his possession, and added that he had sent Waco to watch Pajaritos. "It's ammunition, Captain," he concluded. "De Griego's got ambitious, an' he needs shells."

"You bet he does!" the ranger growled. "Hell's popped over there, all right. Díaz is gone. Madero has a revolution started, and de Griego's gettin' an outfit together. He'll yell . . . *¡Viva la revolución!*' . . . an' claim he's a Madero man, an' make that the excuse for every bloody thing he can do. This was good work, Jim," he commended.

"It was Waco that shot the eagle," Jim reminded. "I thought he'd better watch Pajaritos. We saw a lot of pigeons down there. An *hombre* named Sanchez has got 'em. It looks like this note was meant for Sanchez."

"An' Sanchez didn't get it," Ringold said with satisfaction, folding the note and placing it in his shirt pocket. "If they hadn't got flossy an' used pigeons, we'd still be in the dark. The way it is, we'll be on hand to arrest de Griego when he comes over. He's wanted for everything, from murder on down, an' I only hope he puts up a fight. Where'd you get the spare horse, Jim?"

"Picked him up," was the answer. "I saw him when I was comin' over here." Briefly he mentioned his conjecture regarding the pinto's ownership.

"Likely that's right," Ringold agreed. "All right, Jim. Here we are. Now I've got to get ready to meet *Señor* de Griego." His smile was thin and ominous.

Both men dismounted at the camp. The rangers, clustering about Jim, would have asked questions, but their captain's swift orders sent them scurrying. Ringold was suddenly in high good humor, and his men, taking their temper from him, were equally elated. They had been along the border for some time without action, and they welcomed excitement.

Having told of the news and given orders concerning immediate movement, Ringold returned to Tayler, who stood close by.

"I'll want you along, Tayler," the ranger officer stated. "You and what men you can bring. You've got no objections, have you?"

"Not a one," Tayler answered. "De Griego's been livin' on my beef a long time. I'll be glad to get a shot at him. So will the boys. If you want fresh horses, Captain, I'll have a bunch run in."

"Do that, then," Ringold decided. "We can use 'em."

Tayler hurried away, and Ringold turned again to Jim. "Where will Ibolt meet us?"

"In the creek bottom above town," Jim answered. "How we goin' in, Captain?"

"How does it lay?" Ringold wondered. "I've been down

111

there, but not lately. What would you say, Jim?"

"We could pinch 'em off at the ford, I think," Jim said slowly. "We'd put a few men at this end to hold it down. The rest of us could be over west. There's some breaks there that would hide us. Then we could come down, an', if they ran, they'd be held off from the river, an' the men on this side would cut 'em off."

"I'll look at it when we get there," Ringold promised. "Maybe you're right. That might be the way to do it. Tayler's sent out after the horses. I hope it don't take forever to bring 'em in. I want to get goin'."

He walked away, and Jim, going to his animals, began to pull the pack off the mule. A couple of rangers came to help, and the mule was unpacked and unsaddled in record time. Then Jim unsaddled his own horse and went on to the pinto.

"Might as well take the saddle off this one, too," he commented. "He's been carryin' it long enough."

"You can turn 'em all in with ours," one of the helpers informed him. "We're goin' to throw them into Tayler's horse pasture."

"I'll do just that," Jim agreed.

As they reached the pen, the leaders of Tayler's remuda showed up over the hill, bobbing along at a run.

"Didn't waste any time gettin' 'em," commented a ranger private, standing near Jim. "Sent two men after 'em. Man, I'm sure glad that we're goin' out! I've been plumb bored sittin' around, suckin' my thumb, an' keepin' out of the captain's way. He's sure been ringy lately. Austin's been ridin' him, I guess."

The remuda was penned, and a lanky ranger, using his rope with the facility of a schoolmarm using a pointer, was snaking out horses. As the horses were roped and pulled out, the roper called a name, and a man went forward, carrying a bridle, to claim his mount. Jim, removing the rope from the mule and turning her loose, freed the horse he had ridden that day and turned to the pinto. As he pulled off the bridle of the paint horse, he lifted the mane. There, high on the neck, was a brand: a small picket pin. Jim let the pinto go and stood, holding both bridles.

"Barre!" the roper called. Breaking out of his introspection, Jim walked forward, stopping at a post to hand the pinto's bridle from its top. As he bridled the horse, he examined the men around him. Tayler was there, and with Tayler, standing close, were four others, all of them strangers.

When Jim reached the camp with his horse, he saddled, and then went over to a little congregation of rangers.

"How many men has Tayler got here?" he asked.

"Four, an' a cook," came the prompt answer. "Why, Barre?"

"Nothin' in particular," Jim answered. "I was just wonderin'."

"Anyhow, four is all we've seen," the ranger said. "He's got some more men at his camps, I guess."

"Did you ever know a fellow named Wadell?" Jim asked.

"Stupe Wadell?" the ranger asked in surprise. "Yeah," he agreed, "I know Wadell."

"Ever see him here at Tayler's?"

"No." The ranger shook his head, his face still showing astonishment. "Is Stupe in this country?"

"Mount up, boys!" Ringold, already astride his horse, called the order.

"I saw Stupe at the Crossroads the other day," Jim answered, as he mounted. "Just thought maybe you'd seen him."

"Barre," Ringold called. "I want you."

Jim reined his horse around and rode toward the captain.

Ringold waited until Jim came up, and then started along toward the south. Two by two, the others fell in place to follow, Tayler and one of his men coming immediately behind the captain. From the door of the cook shack the solitary cook watched them go.

"Maybe," Ringold growled, "when I report this, Austin won't ride my tail so hard. They've sure been on it."

Jim repressed a grin. The adjutant general in Austin *had* been riding Ringold then. That accounted for the captain's ill temper. It was always that way. The man in the office rode the man in the field and demanded results.

"They can't ride you if you bring in de Griego," Jim said quietly. "Bringin' him in would be a feather in anybody's hat."

Ringold nodded. "An' we'll get him this time," he said confidently. "Get him sure."

"If nothin' slips, we'll get him," Jim agreed.

Back at the cook shack the cook had left the door. He was minus his apron now, and, spurs on his heels, he walked toward the corral. Not one of the little column, filing along the trail beside the creek, saw him. They were not looking back. Their eyes — as their thoughts — were turned ahead. One of the troop, a youngster barely turned nineteen, assayed a whistle. Stern voices bade him cease. With the setting of the sun the thick dusk of late November descended rapidly. Through that dusk the men rode in silence. In another hour the moon would rise.

Twelve

The Raid

Stupe Wadell sat on a box and looked across the little room to where Fox Lemoine smoked a cigarette beside a stack of cases. Wadell's blank, expressionless face showed no interest in what Lemoine was saying, and betrayed nothing of what was in his mind. Lemoine, his voice high-pitched for a man's, continued his monologue.

"We've got ten cases of shells an' eighteen Winchesters. De Griego wants 'em, an' I think we'd ought to get 'em across to him. I don't like that ranger company down there . . . I don't . . . an' I don't like to keep foolin' with this gun-runnin'. I want. . . ."

Wadell interrupted then, breaking flatly into Lemoine's speech. "We'll move the stuff when Tayler gives the word," he stated. "Not before. Tayler's sendin' it across whenever de Griego's got the money. It's a C. O. D. business."

"But them rangers . . . ," Lemoine repeated.

"You're spooked because Carl was killed," Wadell cut in. "You an' Carl had no business playin' with Barre an' Ibolt. If you'd killed Ibolt, it wouldn't have happened."

"De Griego wouldn't do it," Lemoine growled.

Wadell began to roll a cigarette. "Carl was a fool," he said. "Crazy. He tried to take Barre into camp by beatin' him over the head with a six-shooter. I could have told him that Barre was bad."

"But Barre's got that saddle," Lemoine protested. "We thought we'd. . . ."

"You thought you'd get hold of Barre an' find out if he'd

learned anythin'. That's what you thought when we got young Clark, an' that's what you thought when we caught Chino Joe. It didn't work. Clark didn't tell us anythin', an' the 'breed didn't know." Wadell lighted his cigarette and puffed reflectively.

"Anyhow," Lemoine said sullenly, "I didn't lose my head an' beat 'em to death. I didn't. . . ." He stopped abruptly, lowered his eyes from Wadell's steady stare, and twisted his cigarette back and forth between his fingers.

"Maybe," Stupe suggested, "you ain't satisfied with the way I handle things, Fox."

"It ain't me," Fox Lemoine said swiftly. "But Tayler. . . ."

"Tayler, the fool!" Wadell's voice was still soft, the more sinister for its very gentleness. "He bought a saddle from Waco Ibolt. He thought he was gettin' Howie Clark's old saddle, but Ibolt sawed off another on him. An' Tayler pulled out an' left us behind. He was tryin' to slip it over on us, Fox."

Lemoine threw down his cigarette and got up. "He was with us when we caught the 'breed," he reminded.

"But he wasn't with us when I worked on Dale Clark," Wadell interrupted. "Tayler would have left us to hang, if we'd've been caught. An' we'd have been caught, if I hadn't used my head an' killed Vigil."

There was a moment's pause. "Anyhow, you didn't use your head when we had Clark," Lemoine stated. "He'd have told us, if you hadn't beat him."

"Are you quarrelin' with me, Fox?" Wadell asked gently. "Because if you are. . . ."

"No!" Lemoine's assurance was hasty. "No, it ain't your fault, Stupe. But it looks like we've drawed a blank now. Barre's got the saddle. Dale Clark's dead, an' so is Chino Joe. That mine that old Howie found is lost, I reckon. Nobody will ever find it. An' I saw the ore that they took out of Howie's pockets when Joe brought him home. It was so stiff with wire gold that it wouldn't fall apart when we broke it with a hammer. Howie made a map . . . I know he did . . . an' hid it some place on his saddle, or else why did Chino Joe say that Howie had told him to give the saddle to the kids? That was the last thing Howie said before he died."

"We've still got an ace." Wadell put his cigarette on the dirt floor and crushed it thoughtfully with his boot. "We can. . . ." He stopped. From outside there came the sounds of a traveling horse. Wadell got up. "Here comes the word you've been wantin'," he drawled. "Here's Tayler come to tell us where to take this stuff."

The horse came on, running, then there was the swift stop, an instant's pause, and the door of the room banged open. The cook from Tayler's Hatchet Ranch stood in the doorway, breathing hard, his swarthy face lined with eagerness and anxiety.

"*Señores . . . ,*" he began.

"*¿Que dice, hombre?*" Wadell growled.

The cook spoke no English. Swiftly, as rapidly as his lack of breath would permit, he poured out his story. The rangers were going to Pajaritos. *El Señor* Tayler had told him. There had been a mistake, and Agapito de Griego was coming to Pajaritos to get the ammunition and the guns. Agapito must be warned, or else he would ride into the trap. There had been but time for a word with *Señor* Tayler, then he had come to learn what must be done.

Before the conclusion of the cook's tale, Fox Lemoine had picked up his saddle. Now with the last word of the story spoken, he started toward the door. Wadell halted him.

"Wait!" he ordered. "Where are you goin', Fox?"

"I'll make it across an' keep Agapito on the Mexican side,"

Lemoine answered. "He. . . ."

"You'll stay here," growled Wadell. "I've got an idea."

The cook glanced from one man to the other, not comprehending their words, but reasoning that here was a delay. "*¡Andale, señores!*" he urged. "*¡Andale! Agapito está. . . .*"

Wadell growled — "*¡Cállate la boca!*" — and the native stopped short, his mouth open.

"But . . . ," Fox Lemoine began.

"Let Agapito ride into it," Wadell growled. "We don't owe him nothin'. We don't owe Tayler nothin', either."

"But Agapito . . . ?" Lemoine persisted.

"Look," — Wadell's eyes were narrow — "Tayler's tried to double-cross us once, an' he's sellin' guns an' shells to de Griego so as to get in good. When Agapito is boss on the other side of the border, Tayler figures to deal with him. Why can't we do the same thing?"

Lemoine made no answer.

Wadell, small eyes cunning, continued: "Tayler's gone with the rangers." Then, turning to the cook: "*¿Está el Señor Tayler con los rangers?*"

The cook nodded violently. "*Sí. Está.*"

"Let 'em come together, then," Wadell said callously. "Agapito will see Tayler an' think that Tayler's crossed him an' let him ride into their trap. That'll fix Tayler's hash."

"But suppose Agapito's killed?" Lemoine protested. "An' suppose . . . ?"

"There'll be somebody else for us to deal with if Agapito's killed," Wadell answered, his voice hard. "An' we'll have the guns an' shells to deal with, too. We'll move 'em an' cache 'em some place else. An' we'll get that ace I was talkin' about an' go to Las Palomas."

"The ace you was talkin' about?" Lemoine did not comprehend.

118

"The girl, you fool!" Wadell snapped. "If Dale Clark knew anythin', she knows it, too. An' if we got her, we could trade her for the saddle, couldn't we?"

"The girl?"

"Marilee Clark," Wadell said impatiently. "We can get hold of her. The rangers are gone from the Crossroads. There's nothin' to stop us. We get the Clark girl an' take her over to Las Palomas. If she knows anythin', we'll learn it, an' we can trade her for that saddle. Barre'll give it up, if we got her. An' we'll hide these guns an' shells. We'll use 'em just like Tayler wanted to. We'll trade with 'em, an' Tayler can go to hell."

It took a little time for the idea to sink into Fox Lemoine's shallow mind. He thought about it, gazing at the floor as he considered. Then, suddenly, he looked up. "I'll throw in with you, Stupe," he agreed.

"You're damned right you will!" Wadell answered. "Now then. . . ."

"What about him?" Lemoine jerked his head toward the cook. "He'll tell. He'll say he come here. . . ."

"Him?" Wadell studied the cook with narrowed eyes. "He won't say a word. *¡Ven acá, hombre! ¡Mira los . . . !*" The cook turned his head, obeying the command to "look at the. . . ." Wadell took a smooth step forward, lifting his gun from its holster. The weapon crashed down on the unsuspecting cook's head, and the man staggered, screaming. Again Wadell struck, and then, eyes blazing insanely, he bent above the cook's prone body, striking again and again, and yet again.

"Man alive!" Lemoine reached Wadell and caught his arm. "Don't do that! He's dead, I tell you. He's dead!"

Slowly Stupe Wadell straightened. For an instant he stood glaring at Fox Lemoine, and from those awful eyes Lemoine recoiled.

"We've got to move the boxes, Stupe," Lemoine said. "Remember? We've got to move 'em!"

Gradually the insane light faded from Wadell's eyes. "Uh . . . the boxes?" he said. "Oh! Yeah, we got to move 'em." Ponderously he stepped away from the body, his bloodied gun dangling in his hand.

"Come on, Stupe," Lemoine urged. "Come on, now. Put up your gun an' help me."

"Yeah," Stupe Wadell said, and his eyes were sane once more. "We'll move this stuff an' hide it. An' then we'll go to the Crossroads."

Nate Ringold and Jim Barre, riding at the head of the column through the dusk, considered ways and means. "I wish," Ringold said slowly, "that there'd been some way we could have got that message to where it was goin'. That paper off the pigeon's leg, I mean. Then we might have made a good haul. If we could catch the men runnin' guns from this side, as well as Agapito, we'd have it all cleaned up. The way it is, we'll catch de Griego, if we're lucky. Then whoever takes his place will get hold of the men on this side, an' we'll have it all to do again."

"Captain," Jim said, "who brands a picket pin down in this country? I don't know where the cow brand is set, but the horse brand is on the neck, left side, pretty high up."

"I don't know." Ringold looked sharply at his questioner. "I've never seen that brand down here. There's an outfit brands the picket pin up around the Sweetwater, but that's a way off. Why, Jim?"

"I'm beginnin' to wonder, an' I've got some ideas," Jim answered. "How does the Sweetwater outfit make its brand . . . straight with a circle on the top, or crooked with a circle?"

"Straight," Ringold said. "Ideas about what?"

"They're just ideas," Jim answered vaguely. "It wouldn't do for me to say until I'm sure. Now . . . there's Waco ahead. Under the bank."

The little man came out to meet the troop as it rode up, leading his horse and standing squarely in the trail until the captain reached him.

"It's all right," Waco said, answering Ringold's query. "I laid out on the slope an' watched the place. Nothin' happened. They've penned their goats an' are cookin'. The smell of it like to starved me to death."

"They didn't see you?" Ringold asked, and Waco's answering — "No." — was almost scornful.

"Then I'll slip up an' take a look," the ranger captain announced. "You come with me, Ibolt."

Waco mounted, and the two men rode away. Jim lounged in his saddle, and Tayler came up to sit his horse beside him.

"I don't think we'll have any luck," Tayler remarked. "De Griego's pretty wise. He'll put out a scout to see if his message got through."

Jim, looking through the growing darkness, studied Tayler's face. He could tell nothing from the rancher's appearance, and what Tayler had just said was true. Agapito de Griego might, indeed, send a scout across the river before risking his own important personage. And, if de Griego did come, without first scouting, he himself would stay well behind his followers.

"It's too bad," Tayler said, "that Ringold can't go into Mexico. He could clean up a lot of nests over there. But then, rangers can't cross the border."

"McNelly did," Jim reminded. "An' I've heard of a case or two. . . ." He broke off. There had been more than one occasion when a ranger had unofficially crossed the river. Both Tayler and Jim knew that.

"Ringold said that he was trying to put you an' Ibolt on the muster roll," Tayler stated.

"Did he?" Jim's voice told nothing.

"Yeah. Said that you'd been a ranger, but weren't enrolled now."

"That's right."

Silence fell. Behind the two a man shifted in his saddle, the leather creaking. Away down the line a ranger spoke low-voiced to his fellow.

"Agapito won't come till moonlight," Tayler drawled. "That's a bad crossin', even in the light."

"Not as good as the one farther up?" Jim ventured.

"Better," Tayler answered automatically, and then: "How did you know that there was a crossin' farther up?"

"There had to be."

Again silence fell. A horse stamped, and there was the flick and swish of a tail brushing at some unseen nuisance. A man, chewing tobacco in lieu of smoking a cigarette, spat, and the sound carried crisply.

Then, from the right, there came the splash of horses crossing the stream, and Jim said with relief in his voice: "They're comin' back."

Shadowy forms loomed up at the edge of the creek bank, and Waco's voice was cheerful.

"Guess you got tired of waitin', Jim."

The horses and men were closer now. Ringold's tall body was bent forward, but Waco sat bolt upright.

The men drew to a halt, and Ringold said: "We'll move over to the right. There's a good place. I'll leave four men here." Names followed, and men detached themselves from the shadowy column, forming a little group to the left. "You'll ride down to where the creek bends," Ringold directed them. "Stay there. Close in when we do. Don't let anybody by this way. Drive 'em to the east. The rest of you follow me."

Movement stirred the line of waiting horses. Waco rode beside the captain, and Tayler held his place at Jim's elbow. They went along the trail, broke over the bank, and splashed across the stream.

"Quiet now," Ringold's voice floated back. "No talkin'." The caution was gratuitous. Not one of the men that followed but knew that silence was necessary.

Across the stream the column climbed a bank and ascended a slope. Below the top of the slope Ringold changed direction, skirting the crest, and then as they rounded the end of the hill, stopped. Behind the officer the others checked their horses. Ringold dismounted, and the men following that example slid down from their horses. The ranger captain moved among his men, speaking in a low voice. Then, returning, he touched Jim's arm.

"You an' Ibolt come along," he ordered.

Jim slid his Winchester from its sheath on the saddle. A man took his horse's reins. With Waco beside him Jim followed the black bulk of Ringold's body up a slope and, reaching the top, stopped and lay down, stretching his body beside the long figure of the ranger. Down below, through the darkness, they could see the wink of light.

"We'll wait a while," Ringold whispered.

Time dragged interminably. Behind the three there was an occasional minor sound: the movement of a horse, the faint clink of metal, the rasp of a shifted foot. These spoke of the troop. The men on the ridge top did not stir.

"Jim," Ringold whispered, "I want you to get Sanchez. Get him when we first hit the place, an' keep him. He'll tell us who was to get that message."

Jim grunted his assent to the order. Ringold was wise.

Sanchez was the man with the pigeons, and he would know for whom the message was meant.

"Don't let him get away, now," Ringold cautioned.

The upper crest of the moon, silvery white, came above the eastern hills. Light began to trickle down into the creek bottom. The moon assumed the appearance of a great golden bowl, and now the tops of the flat buildings of Pajaritos were illuminated. It was peaceful down there, peaceful and quiet. To the south the moonlight made the river crossing a thing of silver, with little frosted ripples showing the ford. The moon came on, higher and higher, but still there was no sign of the men from across the border. Waco shifted nervously. Waiting was hard for the little man, hard for them all. Then, in the darkness of the cañon across the river, something stirred, moved, and was still.

"Comin'," Jim breathed. "You want me to get the boys, Captain?"

"Wait," Ringold ordered. "Let 'em get across."

There were horsemen across the river now, a small black knot of them. They paused at the ford, seemingly in consultation, and then a horse splashed into the river, disturbing the silver of its surface. Another followed, and another, and another, until the black clump of riders had changed to a thin line of horsemen in the stream.

The forerunner, reaching the bank, came up toward the buildings, and Ringold's voice rasped in Jim's ear. "Bring 'em up now."

Jim slid back off the ridge and, straightening, ran down the slope toward the waiting men. "They're there!" he announced quietly. "Come on."

About him, men mounted. Bridle reins were thrust into his hand, and he found a stirrup and stepped up into his saddle. Horses and men moved forward, reaching up the slope. Ringold, tall, dim in the shadow below the ridge top, stepped toward them as they came. A man swung a lead horse up beside the captain, and Ringold mounted. Waco, too, was in the saddle.

"Now," Ringold said curtly, "make your line an' follow me. I don't want any of them to get back across."

Again there was movement as the line formed along the slope. Turning his horse, Ringold rode forward again, and behind him the others followed. They reached the ridge top, came down the slope, progressing steadily, the horses walking, only the clink of a shod hoof striking stone, or the creak of a saddle, betraying their presence. Below them, a hundred yards away, Pajaritos lay deserted, the horsemen who had crossed the river, swallowed by the shadows of the little town.

Ringold's arm shot up, and his horse bounded forward. All along the line spurs were thrust home, and with a rattle of rocks and the grind of sliding hoofs the troop charged. And now, from the shadow of a house, flame spurted and a rifle crashed and a man came running from a shed to dive into a shadow. In Pajaritos, guns thudded hollowly, and flame spurted out, and on the slope the rangers, riding now, their horses running, answered that fire and lifted their voices in shouts.

Jim Barre, striking the bottom of the slope, swung north. Sanchez's adobe was at the north end of the town. Waco followed Jim. The others were going straight away now, making for the river, seeking to cut de Griego's men off from the ford. In the little settlement there was shouting and confusion, and a milling of horses as men mounted. Then a rider shot out, making for the river. Clearing the buildings, he rode perhaps fifty feet and toppled from his horse. The horse whirled and came charging back. That much Jim Barre saw, and then no more, for he had reached Manuel Sanchez's adobe.

As he came around the corner of the house, he saw a man run out into the moonlight, fling himself at a frightened horse and, snatching bridle and horn, go up. Waco shouted — "Sanchez!" — and wheeled his horse after the fleeing rider. Jim, too, swung his horse, the animal slipping and almost going down as it turned. Delayed for an instant he pulled his horse up, checking the fall. The animal recovered and broke into full stride, gaining on Waco and the fleeing man. Straight north they went, along the creek, and Jim, overtaking Waco, could hear the small man's shouted curses.

Ahead of Jim his quarry turned in the saddle, looking back, gun tipped, arm lifted. Something smacked the air beside Jim's head, and something else sang shrilly away from beside his horse. Then there was a shock that seemed to check horse and rider in mid-stride, flinging Jim forward over the saddle horn. His saddle had been struck by a shot!

The horse recovered and went on, Jim straightening again in the saddle. From the point ahead, men came riding to intercept the lead man in this chase, and for the first time Sanchez yelled, shrilly, his shout high with fear. One of those men ahead was spurring forward. It seemed to Jim that the two met. There was gunfire, close, immediate, sharp. Then the horses parted, and the man who had come from where the hills reached down to the creek, rocked out of his saddle, to fall spread-eagled to the ground. Jim lifted the Winchester and, reins flying, fired once, twice again, his hand racing on the lever. Up ahead Sanchez seemed to lose balance, to lean farther and farther to the right, until, all balance gone, he toppled slowly, his horse going on alone.

Fighting down his frightened horse, Jim finally brought the animal to a halt. Waco came pounding up and slid to a stop, and from the point ahead the three rangers came, their horses trotting. With a start of surprise Jim realized that quiet had come, that there was no more shouting, no more gunfire. Then the first of the rangers reached him, and in a voice that was curiously flat he said: "He got the kid. Killed him when they came together."

Thirteen

The Saddle's Secret

Jim Barre dismounted. Waco was bent in his saddle, looking down. The three remaining men that Ringold had left at the north side of the area were clustered about the body of their companion. The boy, youngest of all the company, lay face turned skyward, his young countenance singularly at peace.

"He was whistlin' as we rode up here," one of the rangers said slowly. "I made him shut up. Now he won't never whistle. You killed the Mexican, Barre."

Twenty feet distant Manuel Sanchez lay, sprawled on the sand and gravel of the creek bottom. Farther away his horse had stopped and was faced around, and now looked inquiringly at the little knot of men.

"Here comes Ringold," Waco said, and got down from his horse.

The ranger captain, tall on his horse, came up, stopped, and dismounted slowly. For a moment he was silent. Then, his voice level, he announced: "We'll take him back to Tayler's to bury him. He was the only one killed. Nobody else got a scratch."

"It was Sanchez," Jim stated. "Waco an' me made for his house. Sanchez broke out an' caught a loose horse. We were after him, an' he an' the kid came together."

"An' Sanchez?" asked Ringold.

"Dead," a ranger answered.

A slow frown came over Ringold's face. "I wanted him," he said. "He knew who had the guns. "Well, he'll never tell now."

There was a little silence.

Then Ringold said gruffly: "Look after the kid. Catch his horse an' we'll take him with us. Jim, you an' Ibolt come along."

Leading their horses, the three men walked back toward Pajaritos.

In the small settlement the rangers were busy. There were eight bodies laid out in a stark line in the moonlight.

"Two of 'em got away," Ringold said simply. "Do you know any of these men?"

Waco and Jim made a brief inspection. The faces of the dead, some contorted, some peaceful, were unfamiliar to them.

"We don't know any of them, Captain," Waco reported.

"Tayler didn't know 'em, either," Ringold stated. "Agapito didn't come across the river at all. There were four or five stayed on the other side with him. They sloped." His tone was lifeless, all the ring gone from it.

Two rangers came riding in from the east. As they drew rein, one of them announced: "We lost 'em, Captain."

Ringold nodded. Tayler and his men formed a compact body to the right. From this group the rancher advanced a step.

"What are you going to do now, Ringold?" he demanded.

Ringold shrugged. "Go back, I guess," he answered. "De Griego's not coming here again. We're done. An' we have a boy to bury. I wish I could give him a good funeral."

"You could take him to Saunders," Tayler said tentatively.

"Maybe." Ringold was noncommittal.

"What about these here?" Tayler gestured toward the line of bodies.

"Leave 'em," Ringold said sharply. "There's plenty here in Pajaritos to bury 'em. If they don't want to do that, they can throw 'em in the river!" Sudden savagery was in the captain's tone, brought there, Jim knew, by the death of his own man. Ringold's next words confirmed Jim's idea.

"I'll have to write the kid's people. Whetstone is a long ways off."

Waco had moved away, walking across the patches of moonlight and shadow to where a dead horse lay. In the little adobes of Pajaritos, women and children crouched, silent and hidden. Perhaps men were there, too. Certainly, save for the rangers, there was no movement, no sign of life, about the little place.

"Will we leave a detachment here, Captain?" The ranger sergeant had come up to stand in front of Ringold.

"No," Ringold said. "Roust these people out. I'll question them. An' get a fire going."

Men moved to obey his commands. At the door of the nearest house the sergeant beat a tattoo. Brush snapped as it was broken. A match spurted flame, and wood crackled as the fire caught. Waco touched Jim's arm.

"Goin' to take some time," he said. "We might as well loaf."

Together they retired to the side of the nearest house, sat down there, the moonlight drifting across them, and rolled cigarettes. The sergeant was coming now, shepherding a woman and two children ahead of him. They halted by the little fire.

"Don't be afraid," Ringold said gently, speaking in Spanish. "We will not harm you."

"*Señor.*" The woman's voice was tremulous. "*Por. . . .*"

"Don't be frightened," Ringold said again.

The questioning took time. The women were voluble,

frightened, and called upon the saints to protect them. The children did not talk at all, their round eyes, frightened and fearful, staring up at the tall man who spoke so gently to them. Three men, brought from the houses, were sullen, resentful, close-mouthed. With them Ringold was stern, even threatening. But his questions brought only one answer — "¿Quién sabe?" — and the eloquent shrug of shoulders.

The moonlight waned, and only the fire remained. Then, in the east, light touched the hilltops, and Ringold, turning from the last of Pajaritos' inhabitants, spoke to his rangers: "We'll pull out. Get your horses an' mount up."

The order brought movement. Horses were led out and mounted. Ringold, legs widespread, stood watching. When the last man was mounted, he took the reins of his own horse, toed his stirrup, and swung up. Wordlessly he led the way, and behind him the rangers fell into place, riding along toward the north, cold in the morning breeze that blew down the cañon. They passed by the body of Manuel Sanchez, some looking down at it curiously, others without a glance. At the end of the column was a led horse, its lifeless burden bumping as the horse walked.

"We missed," Waco said, riding beside Jim Barre. "We sure missed that time. Agapito didn't come across the Río. He took damn' good care of his hide."

Jim nodded soberly. He was watching Ringold's straight back, the back of a horseman who rode with long stirrups, upright in his stock saddle. But the captain's head was bent. Waco was right. They had missed, and Ringold's head was bent with disappointment. Sorrow, too. Jim Barre knew the captain, knew the almost paternal attitude that Ringold held toward his men. He wished, futilely, that there were something that he could say, something he could do to straighten that bent head.

The sun was well up when camp was reached. Tayler and his men rode on, up from the creek to the ranch house. The rangers dismounted and unsaddled. A fire was kindled and coffee put on to boil.

Ringold disappeared into his own small tent to labor over his report to headquarters at Austin. The other rangers gathered into small groups, waiting for the coffee. When it was ready, they drank, ate a little cold food, and then rested, sprawling out, some sleeping, some talking, all relaxed. Jim Barre and Waco also lay down. They were bone tired, weary after the long hours of wakefulness, the fight and the ride they had made. It was not long until they slept.

It was about one o'clock when they were wakened by a ranger private, who said that Ringold wanted to see them in his tent. Stretching out and yawning away their slumber, they answered the summons.

Ringold was seated in the tent, a board across his knees and a stub of pencil in his hand. He looked up as the two men entered and rested the pencil on the board.

"You wanted us?" Jim asked.

Ringold nodded. "I'm goin' to bury the boy here," he said. "I've thought it over, an' that's the best I can do. I can't ship him home, an' this is as good a place to bury him as the Crossroads. I've sent the supply wagon in to Gaskin's for a casket. He keeps a few in his warehouse. An' I want you two to take some letters in to mail, and escort the wagon back. Will you do that, Jim?"

"Yes," Jim agreed. "We'll go in."

"I'll be through with these letters in a minute," Ringold continued. "I've written the boy's mother an' father, an' I'm pretty near through with my report to Austin. The wagon's already gone. You'll catch up with it."

"I'm mighty sorry about the boy, Captain," Jim said awkwardly. "Maybe if we'd been a little quicker. . . ."

"You couldn't help it!" Ringold's voice was sharp. "Nobody could help it. I thought I'd put the boy in a safe place, but he rode right into it. An' you dropped Sanchez." He lowered his eyes to his writing again. "You'd better get ready to go," he completed, without looking up.

Jim and Waco went out of the tent. Without comment Waco started up from the creek to bring in the horses. Jim waited, and after a time Ringold came from the tent and joined him.

"Here are the letters," he said, passing over two envelopes to Jim. "You needn't stay with the wagon. Just pass it an' get these in the mail an' then look over the coffins that Gaskin's got. Get the best you can. You'll have a little time in the Crossroads. You won't object to that, will you?" A smile lighted Ringold's tired face.

Jim shook his head. He knew now why the captain had selected himself and Waco for the trip. Ringold was harboring ideas about Jim Barre and Marilee Clark. Jim's flush reddened his ears.

"I'm obliged to you for sendin' us," he said honestly. "But there's no need of Waco goin'. I can make the ride an'. . . ."

"I'm puttin' men out in pairs from now on," Ringold interrupted. "Waco won't object to goin' with you."

"No," Jim agreed and smiled. "He won't. If I started off by myself, he'd holler, though."

Waco appeared, leading their horses. He stopped beside Jim and the captain.

"You know," he said, looking at Ringold, "I kind of thought you was pickin' on us at first, but I guess you ain't. It ain't goin' to be no real hardship on Jim to go to the Crossroads." The small man grinned broadly, and Jim flushed again.

"Just get those letters mailed," Ringold directed, and

turned toward his tent.

They saddled, Jim putting the old Mexican tree on Monte's black-striped buckskin back. Then, side by side, lifting their hands in parting gestures to the few wakeful men who watched them go, they rode out of the camp, struck the trail up the creek, and traveled north.

"Ringold," Waco said, after they had traversed perhaps a quarter of a mile, "ain't such a bad fellow, after all, Jim. I wonder what kind of a job he's got in mind for us?"

Jim shook his head. "He'll tell us when he's ready," he said. "Likely he wants us to set up a camp an' trap line farther east, now that he's moved to Tayler's."

"Likely," Waco agreed. "We'll have to go back an' get the rest of our traps, if he does."

"That's right," Jim said.

They rode on through the pleasant afternoon. Some eight miles from the ranger camp they passed the empty wagon, the horses trotting briskly down the road. They spoke briefly to the ranger driving the wagon and, telling him that they would meet him at the Crossroads, rode on ahead. Jim was not thinking of their errand, but rather his mind was occupied with other thoughts. When Ringold's orders had been carried out, Jim would have some time on his hands. He would go to Gaskin's house and talk with Marilee, or if she was in the store. . . .

Waco's excited voice broke into Jim's pleasant musing. "Say," the little man exclaimed, "what's that on your saddle horn? By golly, Jim, you had a narrow miss last night. A slug hit your horn. Did you know that?"

Recalling the sudden shock that had struck him as he pursued Sanchez, Jim bent forward, running his hand along the front of his horn. His fingers struck the rough tear in the rawhide, but he could not see it well. Waco, all interest, had pushed his horse close and was bending to examine the rip.

"Close," he said. "It was sure close. That big old horn done you some good last night, Jim. If you'd been ridin' any other kind of a saddle, that slug would've got you!"

Jim swung down. He could see the tear now, a long gash in the rawhide covering of the horn, just at its top. Once more he ran his finger along the tear. "It sure would've," he agreed. "Hit the horn an' glanced, I think . . . say!" There was amazement in his voice.

"What is it, Jim?" Waco dismounted and stepped up beside Jim.

"Look!" Jim said. "There's metal under the rawhide. Look there!"

At the upper edge of the bullet tear there was a tiny glint, a hint of something other than wood. Waco's strong, stubby fingers lifted the rawhide, bending it fractionally upward.

"There's a plate on top of the horn," he said. "Under the rawhide."

Jim's long-bladed stockman's knife was already in his hand. "We searched this saddle, Ringold an' me," he recalled. "We never thought there was anything but rawhide on the horn. Hold Monte for me, Waco."

Waco obeyed, and Jim's knife circled the rawhide of the horn, cutting through the heavy, hard leather.

The knife was sharp, but the leather was tough. Pulling, lifting as he worked, Jim Barre cut away the rawhide. When he lifted off the cap he had cut, a metal plate was exposed. Dark, oxidized, heavily embossed, it covered the entire top of the big horn.

"Chino Joe must have covered the horn," Jim said. "That must have been it. Now who'd have thought a man would find this? That rawhide looked like it had been there always."

"It's got a screw in the middle," Waco said practically. "Take it off."

Jim opened the shorter blade of his knife, applied the back to the screw, and twisted. With effort the screw turned.

"That's where a man would hide somethin'," Waco said eagerly. "It's the handiest place on the whole saddle."

The screw lifted. Jim removed the knife and used his fingers, pinching down on the sharp edge of the screw. When it came free, Jim placed it in his pocket, slid the knife blade under the metal plate, and pried.

The plate came up, reluctantly, and the top of the wooden horn, rough and discolored, was exposed. As Jim lowered the metal, a piece of paper fluttered out.

"There it is!" Waco's voice showed his excitement.

Jim bent and retrieved the paper.

It was small, folded into a square, and the top was black with the oxidized silver of the horn plate. The two men stood, their heads almost touching as Jim turned the paper in his hands.

"It's all smudged out," Waco said, disappointment in his voice. "Look, Jim."

"Clark must've drawn or written here with pencil," Jim said. "It's rubbed so much you can't make a thing of it."

Unfolded, the paper presented almost the same appearance. On its inner side it was cleaner, but the pencil lines were blurred and meaningless.

"He tried to draw a map," Waco announced. "That's what he did. Tried to draw a map to the mine he'd found . . . with a pencil."

Jim completed the unfolding of the paper. Waco was right. There were traces of lines, blurred and smudged until they were only traces, decorating the paper he held. Two of the squares, those exposed when the paper was folded, were black.

"Now ain't that the devil." Waco growled his disappointment.

Jim Barre turned the paper over. "Yeah," he agreed. "A map to his mine an' . . . look here, Waco. There's writing on this side. In ink!"

Again Waco's head was bent. His lips moved as he read. Then, straightening, he stared at his friend. "That's a bill of sale," he blurted.

"An'," Jim said quietly, "it's made out to Howie Clark an' signed by Leslie Tayler. Clark was buyin' Tayler's interest in their outfit."

Waco nodded.

"Gaskin told me that it was the other way around." Jim studied Waco with narrowed eyes. "He said that Tayler had bought Clark out, but that Dale an' Marilee had never got a cent from the deal . . . that Tayler claimed he'd paid Clark in full an' had the papers to prove it."

Waco met Jim's look, his own eyes narrow. "There's a skunk in the woodpile some place," he growled.

Jim refolded the paper, his movements brisk. "We'll take this on to the Crossroads," he announced. "Right now."

Both men mounted, and Jim replaced the metal cap of the horn, screwing it down. They rode on, talking, conjecture and surmise passing back and forth between them.

"Gaskin will know," Jim declared. "He'll know what to do with this. We'll give it to him."

Glancing at his friend, Waco grinned knowingly. "Yeah," he drawled. "We'll give it to Gaskin. The girl will be there, too. You know, Jim, this oughtn't to hurt you any with her. It ought to make her right fond of you."

Jim's face reddened. "Anyhow," he said, "if Tayler's cheated her, it'll give her somethin' to go on." Suddenly he stiffened. "I think I smell smoke, Waco."

Waco lifted his head and sniffed. "So do I," he agreed. "Somethin' at the Crossroads, I guess. We're pretty near there."

The horses were trotting now, Monte's black-tipped ears working back and forward, his head lifted. Oscar, too, more phlegmatic than the buckskin, seemed to sense something out of the ordinary. Neither rider paid much attention to their horses. The road rounded a clump of live oak, and, beyond the screening trees, sage stretched away.

As they came past the trees, Jim gave one sharp exclamation and then spurred. Monte bounded forward, and Oscar also jumped ahead. Waco's exclamation was lost in the rasp of hoofs on stone. There, across the low growth of sage, was the Crossroads, Gaskin's store and his house, and the little collection of adobes that made up the settlement. From the store a wisp of smoke was still rising, and the walls were black skeletons of rock that reached up to where the roof had been. There was no movement about the adobes, no wide-eyed children to stare at the riders, no women to peer through small windows. Beyond the store, Gaskin's house stood, its two front windows like sightless eyes, its door open and empty, lifeless as the lax mouth of a dead man.

Fourteen

Murder at the Crossroads

Waco and Jim did not halt at the store. One glance was sufficient. Store and warehouse behind it were gutted by the fire. They swept on, stopping at Gaskin's house. Throwing themselves from their saddles, they started toward the porch.

Halfway there, Jim halted. Thad Gaskin, clothed only in a nightshirt, lay face down just at the corner of the porch, his arms flung out as though, in dying, he had reached to pull himself forward. The sand had sucked up the blood from his wounds, and his head, bald and fringed by reddish-gray hair, glistened as the sun struck it.

Kneeling beside the body, Waco lifted and turned it. Neither he nor Jim spoke. There was nothing that they could do for Gaskin. He was beyond all help. Leaving the body, they went into the house.

Gaskin's old hat was still on the hall tree. A glance into a bedroom showed a disordered bed, a pair of trousers, and a shirt lying across the back of a chair, shoes under the bed. They went on. Another bedroom, off the living room, was likewise a scene of disorder. Here, too, the bedding was tangled, as though the bed's occupant had been hauled bodily from it. There were dresses in a closet curtained off from the room. Feminine articles were in array on a bureau.

Jim Barre, standing in the center of the room, cursed slowly, his voice low, hard as glass.

"There's no blood, Jim," Waco said. "Mebbe. . . ."

"Let's look!" Jim broke in on him harshly.

They went on, out of that room into the kitchen. There all was in order, dishes in the cupboard, the stove utensils clean and hanging in their proper places. Nothing had been touched in the kitchen. The two men returned to the living room.

"It couldn't have been de Griego," Jim said slowly. "He was at Pajaritos. This happened early this mornin'. The fire at the store is almost out."

Waco nodded soberly. "Mebbe de Griego sent another bunch across," he ventured. "While he was at Pajaritos, he could have sent a bunch across that upper ford. It could be that way, Jim. Let's see what tracks we can find."

Waco wanted to get his companion out of that house, wanted to get out himself. For an instant, Jim did not respond to the suggestion, then, without a word, he made for the door.

Their own tracks and the sandy soil made accurate sign reading impossible. They scouted around the house, but they could not tell a great deal about what had happened, how many men had made the raid, just where they had come in, or how they had gone out. Coming back to the front, they stopped once more and carried Gaskin's body inside. Outdoors again, they looked toward the adobes of the settlement.

"We'll scout around over there," Jim said. "There's got to be somebody there."

"Mebbe," Waco grunted skeptically. "If there's anybody left, it's because they couldn't pull out."

The two men rode toward the adobes. The first house was tenantless, showing only signs of a hasty departure. So it was with the second and the third. At the fourth house the door was closed, and Waco's earnest beating on the *portal* brought no response. It was Jim, still in the saddle, who saw motion beyond the house and, circling, stopped the woman who was trying to steal away. He dismounted to talk to her.

140

The woman was frightened. She cowered when Jim questioned her, and would not answer. Patiently he tried, again and again, and, gradually gaining assurance that these men would not harm her, the woman spoke.

She had seen the raid, she said. Awakened by the light of the burning store and by shots, she had run to the window. *Señor* Gaskin had come running from his house, and then had fallen, shot down. The men of the adobe settlement had run out, and then fled because the raiders fired at them. There were many raiders, many, many! One hundred, perhaps more. She spread her hands out. And she had seen *Señorita* Clark riding south between two of them. No. The *señorita* did not seem to be hurt. Tied, she thought, and forced to go, but not injured. And then the raiders were gone, and she had gone back to her *mamacita vieja,* who was very old, and who could not move from her bed. The others had fled because they feared that the raiders would come back, but she stayed with her *vieja.*

The recital finished, Waco and Jim stared at each other. The woman had said that there were a hundred, perhaps more, of the raiders. But the tracks, what few they had found, told a far different story. Jim's mouth was a thin, hard line, and his eyes were blue steel points as he looked at the woman again.

"You say they took the *señorita* south?"

"*¡Sí . . . sí!*" The woman nodded violently.

"To Mexico," Waco declared. "That's where they'd go. That's where they come from."

Jim did not answer Waco. Leaving the woman to return to her charge, the two men mounted their horses and rode slowly along toward the west, skirting the east-and-west road that, intersecting with the road from the north, gave the place its name.

"There's where they crossed," Jim said, halting.

In the sandy soil of the road, tracks showed, cutting across the wheel marks.

"Three of 'em. Ridin' abreast," Waco agreed. "That's what she said. Two men an' the girl between 'em."

"But there's just the three sets of tracks." Jim looked questioningly at Waco. "Where are the rest?"

Waco shrugged. "Mebbe they flew," he suggested.

Following the tracks he had found, Jim went south toward the brush. Here at the Crossroads sage grew and coarse chino grass. Farther to the south mesquite and greasewood interspersed with cactus, Spanish dagger, and sotol lifted up.

"You couldn't track an elephant through here," Waco protested. "Dang it, Jim, they took her to Mexico. It was some of de Griego's bunch."

"Maybe," Jim replied. "I . . . you're right, Waco! Look there."

He pointed. On the branch of a mesquite, just where a trail entered the brush, was a wisp of cloth snatched by the mesquite thorns. Jim Barre bent down and detached the cloth carefully.

"Calico," he said. "She dressed before they took her."

"An' this," stated Waco, "is the trail we used when we come from our old camp, Jim. They've headed for the river crossin' by the camp. I think . . . here comes the wagon."

He wheeled, and they loped off toward the approaching teamster.

"What in thunder's happened here?" demanded the teamster.

"A raid," Jim said curtly. "Gaskin's been killed, and they've headed for Mexico with Marilee Clark. You'll have to take word to Ringold. We're goin' to follow 'em."

The ranger got down from the wagon. "Gaskin's dead?" he asked.

"We carried him into the house," Jim said grimly. "You get one of your horses out of his harness and ride back to tell Ringold what's happened. Tell him we're goin' to follow the raiders."

"You say they've got the girl?" The ranger was slow to comprehend.

"Hang it, man!" Jim flared. "I've told you! They've got her. We're goin' to trail 'em while there's some light left. They'll have hit for the crossin' below our old camp. Ringold will know. Tell him we'll either meet him there or leave word for him."

The ranger looked up into Jim's face, started to speak, and then, foregoing the words, moved swiftly to obey the order he had been given. "I'll get the word to Ringold," he said. "I'll burn the hide off this horse gettin' there. How many was there?"

"We don't know," Jim answered. "The woman we talked to said a hundred, but she's clear off. There aren't that many tracks."

The ranger was stripping the harness from the horse now, letting it fall. "You turn that other horse loose," he directed. "I'm gone!"

He slid a long leg across the bare back of the horse he had chosen, settled himself, and gathered up the lines. The horse moved off, increasing its pace.

"Tell Ringold, if we don't meet him, we'll leave word at our old camp," Jim called. The rider lifted his arm in reply.

"I'll turn this horse loose," Jim said quietly, and, unhooking the tugs, he began to strip the harness from the remaining horse. Waco waited impatiently until Jim had mounted again.

They entered the trail where the piece of calico had hung and, with Jim leading, rode steadily along toward the south. Where space and terrain permitted, they trotted their horses, but for the most part their gait was a walk. Now and then a branch rasped against leather. Now and then the riders ducked to go under protruding growth. The brush was thick and the going difficult, but from time to time Jim could see the tracks of the riders that preceded them. When this occurred, he spoke to Waco.

Other than that, the ride was made in silence. Twice Waco tried to start a conversation, and received no response. Jim's face was set grimly, and his eyes pursued the trail and the country ahead. In the west the sun went down, and the gray of evening began to spread across the land.

It was thick dusk when the two men rode down into the hollow that held their old camp. Turning to Waco, Jim made a needless announcement: "Ringold's not here yet."

"No," Waco agreed.

"So we'll wait a while."

Jim stopped Monte. They were beside the shack. Over to the east the ocotillo corral was a dark blotch against the side hill.

"How long?" Waco asked, dismounting and loosening his cinch.

"Hobble 'em, Waco. We might as well let 'em graze."

With the horses cared for, the men seated themselves against the wall of the shack, each cradling a rifle.

"I wonder if Ringold will come?" Waco ventured.

"He'll come," Jim assured him.

"It means goin' into Mexico," stated Waco.

"He'll come, just the same."

Waco dropped the subject. "How in tarnation could de Griego be in two places at once?" he blurted after a time. "He

144

was sure at Pajaritos last night!"

"It was two bunches," Jim said patiently. "Another outfit raided the Crossroads. An' I don't think there was but the two of them."

"Two men made all that trouble?"

"Just two. It would be easy enough. They could fire the store, roust out Gaskin an' kill him, an' get Marilee. If they took a few shots at the 'dobes, the Mexicans would stay inside. It wasn't their fight."

"Mebbe you're right," Waco agreed when he had thought it over.

"An' I've got an idea who the two were," continued Jim. "Lemoine an' Wadell."

"How do you figure that?" Waco was interested.

"Lemoine's horse, the one I picked up, was branded with a picket pin," Jim explained. "The horse that Stupe was riding, when I saw him at the Crossroads, wore a picket pin, too."

"High up? On the left side of the neck?" Waco inquired.

"That's right."

"That's what them horses was branded that I looked at last night," Waco declared. "That's de Griego's brand!"

Silence followed the statement.

"Then Wadell an' Lemoine are in with de Griego," Jim drawled. "That's the way I have it figured, anyway."

"Wadell's hooked up with Tayler some way," Waco said. "Remember, Stupe was ridin' your old saddle, the one I sold to Tayler?" Waco was silent for a while, and then continued. "I'm all mixed up, though. I can't figger this out. What's your idea, Jim?"

"I've got a lot of ideas," was the answer. "I couldn't prove a thing, but I can guess a lot."

"Go on an' guess, then."

"Suppose" — Jim's voice was slow — "that you figure it

this way, Waco. Murry said that there'd been a half-breed hangin' around with Pancho Vigil back in Carver City. Now, suppose that's this Chino Joe who was in Mexico with Howie Clark an' who brought Howie's body back . . . .suppose that the 'breed was broke an' that he hocked the saddle. Then Dale comes to town an' sees the saddle. He'd know it was his dad's. Marilee recognized it the minute she saw it. Dale would hunt around an' find Chino, wouldn't he?"

"I guess that's right," Waco agreed. "Go on."

"Well, Dale finds this Chino Joe, an' they get together. An' Chino is scared, maybe because he's seen some folks he knows. So he an' Dale arrange to meet down in this country, an' Chino pulls out. Dale borrows some money from me to get an outfit together, an' he buys the old saddle. He sent a wire to his sister, remember? An' told her to come an' bring what money she could get."

"Yeah," Waco said. "An' the folks that Chino Joe saw were the Lemoines an' Tayler. Tayler was there. He bought your saddle."

"That's right. Chino saw Tayler, an' he was scared, so he pulled his freight. Dale had to stick around an' wait for his sister. Maybe he figured us in on it. I'd loaned him some money, an' he'd left the saddle with us. We don't know anything about what he figured. Anyhow, these folks from down here . . . the Lemoines an' Tayler . . . catch Dale an' take him to that shack where he was killed. They've got to have help, so they ring in Stupe Wadell. Stupe is a bad *hombre,* anyhow, an' probably the Lemoines knew him. They got Dale in there an' worked on him, and he probably told 'em he didn't have the saddle, an' that the 'breed was gone. Maybe they didn't intend to kill him. I don't know." Jim stopped.

Waco, after waiting a moment for his friend to proceed, said: "This Pancho Vigil is in on it, too. He stays outside for a lookout, maybe. Stupe knows that Pancho might talk a little, so, when the chance comes, he kills Pancho."

"That's right. Now Tayler traces the old saddle and tries to get it. It's supposed to have a map to Howie Clark's mine in it. Remember when Chino Joe came back from Mexico with Howie's body, he said that the last thing Howie told him was to get the saddle to the kids. Everybody thinks that Howie's drawn a map an' put it in the saddle some place. An' there's some mighty rich ore in Howie's pockets."

"An' Tayler can't find the bill of sale he signed when Howie's body is brought back, an' he thinks mebbe that's in the saddle," Waco supplemented. "An' it was, too. You ain't lost it, Jim?"

"I've still got it," Jim assured him.

"All right. Go on."

So now Tayler buys a saddle from you," resumed Jim. "You sacked it all nice for him, an' he'd naturally think that you'd give him the saddle that was worth the least. He didn't open it up to see. But you've crossed him up an' given him my other saddle."

In the darkness Waco chuckled. "I'll bet he was surprised."

"Likely." Jim's voice was dry. "Anyhow, they all get back here, an' Wadell, who is in on it, quits his job an' comes, too. They find Chino Joe an' try to make him tell what they want to know. An' kill him doin' it. An' then you an' me show up, an' I'm ridin' this old saddle."

"So they make another try for it," Waco said.

Jim nodded.

"An' what about the rest of it?" demanded Waco. "Where does de Griego come in?"

"They're runnin' guns to him," Jim said. "I'll bet on it. That's what he came here about the other night when they

147

trapped you, an' the two Lemoines met him here."

"Only one of the Lemoines left, though," Waco growled. A pause, and then: "If Tayler's in on the gun runnin', how come he went along last night? Why would he do that?"

"He couldn't help himself," Jim answered. "Ringold told him to come. But I'll bet Tayler sent word to de Griego not to be at Pajaritos, but de Griego didn't get the message."

"That could be," Waco assented. "An' now, Jim?"

"An' now" — Jim's voice tightened and grew hard — "they've made a last stab at it. They've got Marilee an' taken her into Mexico. To de Griego's place. Las Palomas, they call it."

Silence came after the statement, both men staring off into the dark.

"An' we're goin' to get her out," Jim said slowly. "When the moon comes up, I'm goin' across. You'll stay here, Waco, an' tell Ringold what's happened."

"Like the devil I'll stay here," retorted Waco. "When you cross the river, so do I. Maybe she's your girl, but I'm goin' along."

There was no arguing with Waco when he used that tone. Short of being restrained by physical force, Waco would cross into Mexico when Jim Barre crossed. And Waco had said: "Maybe she's your girl." Looking out at the velvety blackness that was spread before him, Jim pondered the words. Waco was right. Jim had known women in his life, had danced with them, and flirted with them and admired them, but never before had he experienced the feeling that gripped him now. Win or lose, live or die, no matter what happened, as far as Jim Barre was concerned Marilee Clark was his girl, and he knew it.

"Ain't the blasted moon ever goin' to rise?" Waco growled, breaking into Jim's thoughts.

"It always has, Waco," his friend answered quietly.

Waco thought about that. Then: "Mebbe this is the night it misses. There's always got to be a first time," he said moodily.

Fifteen

Las Palomas

It seemed as though Waco's suggestion might prove true. Time stretched on and on. Finally, in the east, a faint glow appeared, becoming gradually brighter, augmenting the starlight. The moon tipped up over the eastern horizon, a moon with a big chunk bitten out of it.

"Ringold ain't here," Waco observed, as the moon slid slowly toward its zenith.

Jim Barre was on his feet. Ringold had not come, but impatience made waiting longer impossible.

"We'll have moonlight till mornin'," Jim said. "We might as well go, Waco."

Carrying their bridles and the rifles, they went out to the horses. In a few minutes they had the hobbles off the animals' feet and were ready to ride.

"We said," Jim announced when they reached the shack again, "that we'd leave word here, if Ringold missed us. I guess we'd better do it, Waco."

"Yeah," said the other. "How'll we leave it?"

Jim had no answer ready. Neither of them had pencil, paper, or anything that could be used.

"The letters," Jim said suddenly. "Stick 'em up in the wall of the shack. He'll know we've been here." He did not wait for Waco's agreement, but, acting on his own suggestion, wedged the two letters Ringold had given him into a crack where they stuck out prominently.

"He can't miss that," Waco declared.

"Well, then," Jim said, "let's go!"

He mounted the buckskin once more and, leading the way, rode toward the river. Behind him, Waco grumbled at the amount of time that had been wasted.

It was not hard to find the trail that led down to the river, nor was it hard to make the descent. The horses, refreshed, were sure-footed enough, and, heads lowered, they picked their way down the rocky path. At the bottom of the cañon, on the little shingle beside the river, Jim made a discovery. There were horse tracks, comparatively fresh, entering the stream. He pointed them out to Waco.

"If we didn't think they'd come this way, we wouldn't be here," Waco said loftily. "Of course, they crossed. What bothers me is where we come out on the other side." So saying, he slid the Krag from its scabbard and, holding it in front of him, pushed Oscar into the ford. Jim, also removing his saddle gun, urged Monte forward.

As though it were his right, Monte pushed ahead, feeling for footing and picking his course. The horse bore downstream, and then, as the water deepened and sand sucked at his feet, refused to go farther. Jim used his spurs, and Monte, turning against the current, went on again, Waco following. The water deepened, came almost to the saddle skirts, and then began to shallow. Puffing, Monte came out on the southern bank. Jim replaced his rifle, and the grulla came up beside Monte.

"Bueno," Waco commented.

Now the horses took the trail up the slope, climbing vigorously. When they reached the top, Jim stopped, and again Waco came up beside him. The horses blew softly, not at all distressed by the climb. Looking out over the moon-swept country, Jim sought for landmarks.

"Just whereabouts," Waco drawled, "is this Las Palomas we're lookin' for? You got any ideas?"

"It's some place south an' east of here," answered Jim. "It's got to be some place between here an' the Pajaritos crossin'. That's all I know."

"There might be ten ranches between here an' there," Waco pointed out. "That's quite a scope of country."

"No." Jim shook his head. "There's just one place that I've ever heard about. That's Las Palomas. We'll follow this trail, Waco. It'll take us there."

"Mebbe," Waco said skeptically. "Go ahead anyhow."

The trail from the crossing led up a long draw and then bent left. Coming out of the draw, crowning the eastern ridge, the men had a view of a broken, brushy country that stretched away. To the south and east the Sierra Ponces marched majestically, and north and east, across the river, the Chisos lifted jagged peaks against the sky.

The trail wound in and out, threading through the brush, dropping into arroyos, climbing ridges.

"Here," Jim Barre announced finally, "is a wagon road. It'll go to Las Palomas, Waco."

"We'll see," his friend answered.

Riding side by side, following the road, Jim and Waco were silent. Then before them rose a long slope, and Jim spoke again. "Las Palomas will be on the other side of that," he declared.

"If it ain't on the other side of the next one," Waco retorted.

Jim grinned. It was good to be riding along with Waco, listening to the little man refute every suggestion. Waco was all right!

"We've come far enough to be in Mexico City," the little man growled.

They were almost at the crest of the rise now. The road twisted around a heavy growth of mesquite, turned back to the east, and there on the ridge top Jim and Waco stopped. Below them, farther to the east, a little settlement lay in the hollow formed by the ridge they occupied and another rise.

"That's Las Palomas," said Jim.

"Yeah," Waco agreed dryly. "They got its name on a sign. Got 'Welcome To Our City' hung up, too. Now what, Jim?"

"Now," said Jim thoughtfully, "I'll go down an' scout around a little."

"You mean we'll go down an' get ourselves killed," retorted Waco. "All right, let's go."

"One man," Jim began, "wouldn't make as much noise as two. You'd. . . ."

"The dogs they got down there will bark at one man just as quick as they'll bark at a dozen," Waco refuted the argument curtly. "Go ahead."

"*Be* stubborn, then!" Jim said, and started down the slope.

They had a good view of the settlement below them as they rode. There was one big place, surrounded by a wall with a single closed gate. Inside the wall there were houses — long adobes that were low and squat and that made black shadows. There were corrals about the place, outside the wall, and sheds, too. Mixed with these were other adobe dwellings.

"A regular walled city," Waco said low-voiced. "I'll bet there's a hundred men around here. An' more than a hundred dogs."

"Agapito de Griego," Jim drawled, "will live in the big place. The one with the wall around it. An' that's where Marilee will be."

"So?" Waco said.

"So I'll try to get in there," Jim continued. "Look, Waco . . . if we get separated, try to make it back up to where the road jogged. I'll try the same thing. We'll meet there."

153

Waco thought that over. "We'll meet in hell," he commented. "Right at the front door. That's where we'll meet. Of all the fool ideas a man ever had, this is the worst. We've got no more chance than a bartender has of goin' to heaven. Look at them horses in the corral. Why, there's fifty head anyway!"

"You could go back up to the turn an' wait," Jim suggested. "You could. . . ."

"Who said anythin' about goin' back?" Waco cut in brusquely.

Jim said no more on that subject.

At the bottom of the slope they stopped their horses. Here, in the valley between the ridges, the brush was not so thick. Between their halting place and the houses, clumps of mesquite grew dark and heavy, with some greasewood interspersed throughout the mesquite. Coming down the slope, Jim and his partner had quit the road, making their approach through the brush. The road was too open, too exposed.

"We'll have to take our horses," Waco whispered. "I ain't goin' to be caught afoot."

Jim nodded. Looking across the two hundred yards that separated him from the first house, he planned his approach.

Waco dismounted, his saddle creaking. "We sure can't ride in," he said.

Jim assented to the statement by also dismounting. "Try to get to the big house," he directed. "I'll try, too. If we get in, maybe we can surprise 'em, find Marilee, an' get out. Remember, the jog in the road is where we'll meet. I wish you'd go back there, Waco, an' wait for me."

"Just keep on wishin'," his partner said grimly.

There was nothing you could do about Waco. Jim gathered his reins firmly in his hand and stepped out.

They had no difficulty in crossing the first fifty yards. Moving swiftly, Monte following willingly enough, Jim Barre made the shelter of the first clump of mesquite. Waco, too, reached that vantage point with the grulla. The next twenty-five yards were no more difficult, nor was the next small journey. Now, with perhaps a hundred yards between himself and the first house, Jim conceived an idea. Thrusting his reins toward Waco, he whispered sharply.

"Hold them."

Automatically Waco grasped the reins, and Jim, grinning at his trick, whipped around the edge of the clump of brush and ran for the next. Leading two horses, Waco could not follow. He was anchored.

Running, Jim reached the next stop and crouched. He could imagine how Waco must feel, and what the little man was saying. Waco would be a way beyond the boiling point. A puff of wind, gentle and cold, blew against Jim's back, and he left his shelter to make his next run. Somewhere ahead a horse whinnied, a long bugle-like blast, and almost immediately a dog began to bark. Jim reached a mesquite clump, ran from it, and stopped almost against the wall of the nearest house, crouching in the black shadow.

The first dog was joined by another, and then another. Crouching in the shadow, Jim scowled and swore under his breath. He had known there would be dogs. It was axiomatic — one house, one dog . . . sometimes two dogs. Now that the barking had begun, Jim did not like it, even though it was to be expected. All through the settlement the dogs, now aroused by each other, were lifting their voices with the rhythmic regularity of so many Chinese firecrackers.

Jim moved along the side of the house until he came almost to the end of the shadow. His Colt was in his hand, and, crouching there, he waited. Somewhere behind him, but close by, a door opened, and a man's voice, speaking wrathful Spanish, bade the dogs be still. A thud and a yelp followed the command. Jim grinned. One dog had been well kicked.

The door banged shut, and Jim, slipping from the friendly shadow, ran across an open space and dropped to shelter beside the rock wall of a corral. The movement brought greater attention from the dogs. Crouched beside the corral wall, Jim heard a low growl almost in his ear. He struck with the Colt, felt the gun hit something, heard a yelp of pain, and then struck again. Yapping shrilly, the dog ran from the shadow.

This, thought Jim grimly, was not so good. In fact, it wasn't good at all. Other doors were opening now and querulous voices were calling, demanding to know what was the trouble, what was happening. All of Las Palomas was waking up, and he, Jim Barre, was right in the middle of it. Something had to be done and soon. He straightened beside the wall and, back bent so that his head would not appear above the stone, walked along its length.

Reaching the end, Jim stopped again. Opposite him, perhaps twenty feet away, was the high rock wall around the house that he had selected as Agapito de Griego's. Jim computed distance, and, holstering the Colt, he jumped from the shadow of the corral and ran toward the wall.

When Jim had thrust Monte's reins into Waco's hand, the little man accepted the charge without realizing at once just what had happened. Finally aware of the thing Jim had done, perhaps two seconds after Jim had run for the next shelter, Waco let the reins drop.

Monte promptly tossed his head and moved along the length of mesquite bush. Monte was spoiled, a pet, and he knew just exactly what to do about trailing reins. To get along with an outfit like that, a horse just had to turn his head and move sideways. Monte savvied the whole game. The instant after Monte moved, Waco realized that he had made a second mistake. Regardless of cost, he should have held onto Monte. Transportation was a vital factor, and a man on foot in country like this was helpless. Stifling a curse, Waco went after the horse, his own reins gripped firmly. Monte surveyed Waco's approach, tossed his head, and moved along a little farther behind the mesquite.

"Whoa," Waco commanded, as loudly as he dared.

Monte watched Waco and cocked his ears to see if the little man really meant it. Oscar, seeing no particular reason for hurrying, hung back. Grimly Waco towed the grulla along.

"Whoa," he ordered again.

At that moment, in sleeping Las Palomas, a horse nickered and dogs began to bark. All the dogs in the world and two more were raised, if noise was any indication. Monte walked out from the shelter of the mesquite and stopped. His very pose showed how pleased he was.

"You crazy buckskin goat!" Waco swore, his temper completely gone. "I'll . . . whoa, damn you!"

Cautiously he advanced from behind the mesquite. Monte went a little farther away. Waco stopped, and Monte stopped. Waco glared at the horse. There was a fresh fusillade of sound from the dogs.

"Got the whole place stirred up," Waco announced, speaking of Jim Barre. "Of all the fool, crazy things a man ever done, this is the worst. Of all the lousy tricks. . . ." For a few seconds he traced the pedigree of Jim Barre, mixing Monte's pedigree and characteristics liberally with his master's. Concluding with another — "Whoa." — he walked toward the buckskin again, Oscar still hanging back on the reins. Monte cocked his ears and trotted around the end of the mesquite clump.

It wouldn't do. It just wouldn't do at all to have that loose horse circulating around. Waco knew it. He knew, too, that on foot he could not catch Monte. Monte would play tag with him all night and enjoy the game. But on horseback a man could ride right up to Monte and catch those reins. With a grim face, Waco turned to his grulla and, twisting out a stirrup, mounted. This brought his head above the top level of the mesquite and made him a very prominent target — too damned prominent, and Waco knew it.

Against the little man's middle the Colt he had taken from Carl Lemoine rubbed coldly. Under his right leg the box magazine of the Krag carbine made an uncomfortable bump, and in various pockets of brush jumper and pants the weight of nearly a full box of .45s and of more than a box of .30–40 shells for the Krag weighted him down. He was a veritable arsenal on the move, and he stuck out, he realized uncomfortably, like a sore thumb. The only salvation in the whole deal was the fact that so far nobody was around to witness his performance.

Urging Oscar forward, Waco started after the buckskin. Monte, looking back, reins trailing, walked sedately toward the houses. Once more Waco swore. If this was going to be done at all, it had to be done quickly. He urged Oscar to greater effort, and the horse loped. Monte broke into a trot, and from the nearest house a dog charged out, barking and snarling.

Monte did not like dogs. He swung his head, saw his attacker, and, squealing, wheeled and kicked the dog into perdition. The dog howled as Monte's big black hoofs struck and disappeared into the shadow of the house. From that same shadow a man said, his voice conveying his astonishment: *"¡Por los vientres de . . . !"* The exclaiming gentleman got no further. Seeing Waco, he squalled like a frightened cat.

Monte was thoroughly angry — for any horse would lose

his temper under such circumstances — and, seeing Waco bearing down upon him, wheeled and cantered in between the houses.

The man who had squalled was apparently not unequipped for emergencies. Flame spouted in the shadow of the house, and the thunder of a short gun split the night. Waco, with no time on his hands for such foolishness as shooting, went past the house, hauled up, fighting Oscar around, and started back the way he had come. Some place in the middle of Las Palomas, Monte was dragging his bridle reins. And some place in there was Jim Barre. About the only thing that Waco could do was hope that the two of them would get together.

Already voices were calling back and forth. The dogs had redoubled their efforts. The man who had first come out to inquire into things was persistently shooting his Colt and making the vicinity unsafe for everybody.

Spurring Oscar, Waco swept past the back of the house and made for the open. Beyond the third mesquite, close to the beginning of the slope, he pulled the grulla to a halt. He hit the ground the instant he stopped the horse, knowing that mounted he was a good target, while on foot he would seem to anyone who watched to disappear. Holding bridle reins in one sweaty hand and gripping his Colt with the other, he approached the end of the mesquite clump, and peered around. Surely, with all that going on in there, Jim would leave. Las Palomas was buzzing like an angry hive of bees. Lights were appearing. Many men were shouting now and running back and forth. And, unless he wished to desert his foolhardy partner, Waco would have to stay where he was. If Jim Barre escaped from that tumult, he was going to need transportation, and need it badly. And Oscar was at this point the only transportation available.

Jim Barre was halfway between corral and wall when trouble broke out behind him. He heard a man scream, and there followed a shot. He heard the dogs redouble their efforts, and then came more shots. Jim did not stop in his run, but struck the wall, caught its top, and, finding a toe hold in its rough surface, went up and over. Landing sprawling on the inner side, he rolled back until he was against the wall, and there, in the shadow, remained motionless.

All about him Las Palomas was coming to life. Lights began to blossom, and voices called. In front of Jim a light showed in a house, and a door opened. A man shouted, inquiring as to the cause of the disturbance and, receiving no answer, yelled again. As Jim could see by moonlight, another man, clothed only in a pair of trousers and carrying a rifle, ran across the courtyard to the gate.

Someone shouted: *"¡Allá está!"*

A man with a rifle fired a shot.

Then a bellowing voice from the big house began to roar orders.

Jim stayed very still.

The man with the big voice had authority. De Griego, Jim guessed his identity. There was turmoil outside the wall, a cacophony of shouts and screams and barking dogs, punctuated with an occasional gunshot as some enthusiast thought that he saw an attacking force. But inside the wall, order began to reign. De Griego, if he was the man with the big voice, was getting results.

A little knot of men formed between Jim and the house, blocking out the lighted door. Then that knot dispersed, running toward the gate. The gate was forced open, and the men were gone. Jim heard the thunder of hoofs as horses stampeded across a corral, and then for perhaps five minutes there was comparative silence. True, the dogs still barked, and women and men called back and forth, but the hysteria was gone.

At the end of the five minutes, Jim heard the pound of horses' hoofs again. This time it was regular, gradually diminishing, sweeping away. Those men who had run through the gate were gone, pursuing someone. Waco, Jim guessed. Momentarily a pang of anxiety swept through his mind. Then, lifting himself, he got up and stood beside the wall. If they had gone after Waco, he, Jim Barre, could not help. There was nothing he could do. And now was just as good a time as any to go into that big house, the door of which was opened so invitingly. With a hitch to his cartridge belt and gun gripped in his sweaty palm, Jim walked forward. He had come here for Marilee Clark, and, if she was inside de Griego's house, he'd get her.

Sixteen

Ringold's Arrival

Out behind the big mesquite Waco waited. He held Oscar firmly and, by peering around the end of his shelter, had a good view of Las Palomas. What he saw was not pleasing. In the moonlight Las Palomas resembled nothing so much as a big nest of hornets that had been disturbed. Watching the activity, seeing the lights appear, listening to the shouting and the spasmodic gunfire, Waco cursed Jim Barre and all Jim Barre's workings. The only satisfaction Waco received, the only thing that helped at all, was the fact that Jim had not been taken. Waco knew that. If Jim was captured, if he was killed, that querulous shouting would change to a roar of triumph, and the aimless running about would stop while men converged on their trophy. So far, Jim was all right.

"They'd *ought* to kill the dog-goned fool!" Waco growled. "They'd ought to. But they ain't got him so far." He pushed his head a little farther beyond the sheltering mesquite, so that he had a better view.

Now, apparently, some order was coming to the chaos. The aimless running had stopped, and the shouting had died down. The dogs were holding their own, all right, making the night a misery of noise, but the dogs' masters were evidently concentrating in one place. What this development foretold, Waco did not know, but he was not long left in doubt.

A little parcel of horsemen appeared at the edge of the settlement and stopped. Waco retreated behind his screen. He wished devoutly that there was a hole for him to hide in. The moon was fairly high, and the shadows were pretty thin. And if those riders came on, if they saw him, Waco knew that he'd have to save his own hide and let Jim Barre attend to everything else. He heard a command, heard the horses start, and crouched behind the mesquite. Maybe, just possibly, they'd pass him by.

No such luck! The riders were coming straight toward the mesquite that sheltered Waco. Like a rabbit that at first tries to avoid detection by remaining utterly quiet, and then seeks safety in flight, Waco went up into his saddle and spurred the grulla. Oscar came out from behind the mesquite and started up the hill, running low, belly almost touching the ground as he earnestly put distance behind him.

For a quarter of a mile Oscar was mighty fast, just as good a horse as a man would want to straddle. But there was more than a quarter of a mile between Oscar and the ridge top. Waco turned his head to see how the other boys were coming, saw that they were coming too blamed good, and then, bending low, he paid strict attention to his riding. Behind him guns cracked viciously, and in the air around Waco and the fleeing Oscar little angry hornets buzzed. Once more Waco ventured a hasty glance. The riders behind him were stringing out, the varying speed of their horses and their varying degrees of horsemanship making themselves felt.

It must have taken Oscar a full minute to reach the ridge top. Waco was carrying no stop watch, and did not know his time for the distance, but he would have bet that the minute was a full hour. And there was no respite even then. Beyond the ridge top was a lot of country, and Waco and the grulla hunted it, bearing off toward the south, where thick brush made promise of some shelter. But there was considerable open space between Waco and the brush, and, looking back for the third time, he saw the first of his pursuers crown the ridge and come on. Oscar was beginning to slow in his stride,

163

and Waco knew it was certainly time to do something about the men who followed him, time to discourage their enthusiasm. Glancing back again, he estimated distances. His Colt was still gripped in his sweaty hand, and his brief survey showed that the foremost pursuer had outdistanced his fellows by a full hundred yards.

"Now, god damn you," Waco swore, "let's see you sit down!" He straightened in his saddle, thrust his feet forward, and pulled up sharply. Oscar, who had cut out many a cow, planted his hind feet, squatted, and slid, coming around to the right. From the top of the grulla, his gun platform almost motionless for the moment, Waco shot three times, as fast as he could cock hammer, aim, and pull trigger.

The foremost pursuer had not been prepared for this type of action. It took him completely by surprise. This was an astonishing thing — as astonishing as a fox that, pursued by hounds, turned and attacked the first of them. The man behind Waco tried to check, tried futilely to turn, his mount. He was within twenty yards of Waco when the third shot was fired. Throwing his arms wide, the rider tipped back in his saddle and, swaying to the side, slipped down. Waco Ibolt, unaware that he had placed a period at the end of Fox Lemoine's career, wheeled the obedient Oscar to the left once more and, spurring, went on toward the heavy brush, reached the first opening in the growth, and turned the grulla west again.

Oscar was blowing heavily. As the brush swallowed them, Waco slowed from frantic run to slower lope. The grulla kept the pace, threading his way through the growth, branches and thorns catching at horse and rider, tearing cloth and cutting flesh. Stubbornly Oscar kept on, but behind the horse and rider the shooting had stopped and men were calling back and forth, lifting their voices in inquiry. Where shin oak and live oak grew thickest, Waco stopped and waited, listening alertly.

How long Waco sat there he did not know. He could hear the pursuing party work past at some little distance. They were persistent devils, but the thing that had happened to their leader had to some extent dampened their ardor. They beat the brush, back and forth, but they stayed together in one compact group, not daring to fan out and cover a wider spread of country. Waco heard them, heard one angry voice command that they spread out, but he did not see them. He waited until the sounds died away, and the night was quiet, and then carefully brought the grulla out of concealment. There was just one thing remaining for him to do. Go back to the turn of the road and wait for Jim. If Jim got out of Las Palomas, he would expect Waco to be there where the road jogged around the mesquite. So, deliberately, Waco rode north.

He struck familiar country in perhaps fifteen minutes of riding. Before him were the Chisos, dim in the moonlight. Somewhere below was the road, and to his right was the long ridge, from the top of which he and Jim Barre had first seen Las Palomas. Quartering across the country, Waco looked for the road, and then, ahead of him, he heard movement. Instantly he stopped and listened.

The road lay before him. Down somewhere on that road, horses were traveling. It was, so Waco believed, his pursuers, returning to Las Palomas. He listened intently, ready to turn and run again. Metal rattled faintly. Horses' hoofs plopped steadily on hard ground. And the sweetest of all sounds, a drawling Texas voice commented: "Dog-gone, how far is it, anyhow?"

Waco leaned forward. "Hey!" he called cautiously. "Hey, down there!"

The sound of movement stopped. Someone gave an astonished grunt. Then, distinctly through the brush, a voice queried: "Who in blazes are you?"

"Ibolt!" Waco answered, and rode forward.

When he reached the road, he could see plainly enough the men he had stopped. Nate Ringold, tall and straight, sat his horse at the head of a little column of men. "Where's Barre?" Ringold demanded as Waco came up.

Relief flooded Waco. Momentarily all the tightness drained out of him. His shoulders slumped and his voice shook a trifle as he made answer. "Jim went into Las Palomas. He ain't come out."

The ranger's face was stern and his voice was hard as he said: "You couldn't wait for us. You had to try it alone, didn't you? What's happened?"

"Jim went in," Waco answered. "I've had a bunch chasin' me."

"You couldn't wait," Ringold said again heavily. "Barre's still in there?"

"I think so," Waco told him.

"How far is it?"

"Just over the rise."

"Come on, then," Ringold ordered. "Ride with me, Ibolt."

Waco fell into place beside the captain as the little column moved forward.

They talked as they rode, Waco Ibolt and Nate Ringold. Ringold's questions were sharp and harsh, and Waco's answers carried no more words than necessary. He told the captain of waiting at the old camp, of crossing the river, of how they had approached Las Palomas, of the trick that Jim had played on him, and of his subsequent flight. By the time he had finished, they were almost at the top of the rise, and

Ringold halted his men.

"You think that Jim was hurt?" the ranger asked.

"Not when I left," Waco answered. "I don't think they'd found him. But there's a thousand dogs down there. If Jim ain't been caught or killed, it's a miracle."

Ringold chewed the end of his mustache. "We come over after that girl," he said. "You two fools. . . ." Ringold broke off abruptly.

"Yes, sir," Waco agreed penitently.

Ringold continued to chew on the corner of his mustache. "We'll take a look," he said finally. "You boys stay here." With that order given, he moved his horse ahead along the road, Waco riding beside him.

Just at the crest, they stopped. Here, where the road jogged around the mesquite, they could look down the slope into the valley below. Lights still burned in Las Palomas, and small noises and the sound of distant barking floated across to them.

"How does it lay?" Ringold asked tersely.

Waco described Las Palomas as well as he could. "There's one big place in the middle, with a wall around it. Jim thought that would probably be de Griego's place."

"Likely," Ringold said, and then, turning his head: "Come on up, boys." The men moved along the road, and tersely Ringold gave orders. "We'll take it easy down the hill. When we hit the bottom, we'll charge. There's a big house with a wall around it in the middle of the place. That's where we want to go. Hit right for it. The idea is to get in, look for the girl, an' get out again without gettin' shot. All right, we'll. . . ."

"What about Jim?" Waco demanded. "He's in there afoot. He. . . ."

"He went in on his own hook." Ringold's voice was harsh. "Let's go, boys!"

Once more the tall captain started his horse, riding deliberately down the slope. For an instant Waco hesitated, then, urging his grulla, he caught up.

It seemed impossible, but the riders were undetected as they came down the hill. They made no particular effort at concealment, merely refraining from conversation as they rode. At the bottom of the slope Ringold looked back, and then, sure that his men were in place, struck a trot toward the dark loom of Las Palomas. For perhaps fifty yards the gait was a trot. Then, from the buildings ahead, a yell went up. Instantly Ringold lifted his horse from trot to run.

In Las Palomas a shot rang out, and then another, and another. And now the men behind Ringold answered that fire and began to yell. Before them men scurried away like congregated mice that flee from a pouncing cat.

"The gate!" Waco shouted. "There's the gate!"

Ringold swung his horse to the left. The gate in the rock wall was open, and the men went dashing through.

In the courtyard beyond the gate Ringold swung down. His horse stood, anchored by trailing reins, as the tall captain, gun in hand, ran toward the house. Waco, too, was down, and another ranger had dismounted.

Running toward the house, Waco shouted: "Jim! Jim! Where are you?" He reached the porch. The door was open, and Ringold was inside. Waco, going through the door, bumped shoulders with the ranger private who had followed his captain. Just inside the door both men halted.

The room was lighted. Candles were burning in a candelabra on a long table. Chairs stood beside the table, and, across from the outside door, another opening gaped blackly. Ringold was across the room, almost at this second entrance. Aside from the captain, the room was empty.

"Marilee!" Ringold raised his voice. "Are you here, girl?"

"Jim!" Waco called.

The shouts reverberated in the long room. Somewhere in the back of the house, a woman shrieked. The ranger private, snatching the candelabra from the table, followed Ringold into the hall. Waco still shouted for Jim.

Back along the hall went the three. A single candle gave fitful illumination in the kitchen, but they found no one in the kitchen, no one in the adjoining rooms. Whoever had screamed must have fled the house.

Ringold wheeled to face his two companions. "Back!" he ordered. "By glory, I'll find her, if I have to take this place apart."

They made their way back along the hall. Dark doorways gaped at them from either side. Into these doorways the ranger private thrust his candles, illuminating the rooms. There were signs of occupancy in the rooms, clothing strewn about, disturbed covers on the beds, confusion which showed that recent occupants had hastily departed, but there was no one to be found. No Marilee Clark or Jim Barre.

Back in the big room which they had first entered, Ringold stopped. The private, holding the candles high, was at the door of the hallway. A ranger, running from the courtyard, reached the outer door and halted.

"They're gettin' together," he reported breathlessly. "They're gangin' up. The boys are holdin' the gate, but they'll be comin' over the wall in a minute."

"Jim?" Waco demanded, moving forward. "Did you find . . . ?" He stopped. The ranger at the doorway was watching Ringold. Waco, too, looked at the tall man. Ringold's face was working, emotion changing its pattern. The ranger who held the candles took long steps and replaced the candelabra on the table.

"She's not here!" Ringold said. "We'll. . . ."

"Cap'n!" The ranger private who had held the candelabra

on their search of the house barked the word. Ringold wheeled toward him. The man, one hand still on the candelabra, was leaning forward over the table. He straightened as Ringold looked, turned his head, and snapped one short sentence. "There's a dead man here."

Ringold strode toward the table. From the door the ranger came hurrying, and Waco Ibolt, heart in his throat, ran toward the table. Was it Jim?

At the end of the table he stopped. There, behind the table, a man lay, sightless eyes staring toward the ceiling. The candlelight, flickering down, showed a dark face, a black mustache over the gaping mouth, lifeless eyes catching the light. Waco's heart flopped back into his chest again.

"De Griego," Ringold said slowly. "Agapito de Griego. I know him. How . . . ?"

"Jim!" Waco said again. "He's been here, an' he's got the girl."

For an instant Ringold stood peering down across the table end, then, lifting his head sharply, he rapped commands. "Outside! We'll go!"

For the first time Waco was aware of the firing from the courtyard, the spasmodic explosions of guns. Ringold was striding toward the door. The other rangers were also moving to the outside. Once more Waco looked at the vacant, upturned face, and then he, too, turned and ran toward the doorway. Jim Barre was not here. But he had been here and left his sign. It was time to go.

Seventeen

Flight from Las Palomas

Coming across the long porch of Agapito de Griego's house in Las Palomas, Jim Barre kept well to the left of the one door. It was just as well not to walk directly into anything. When he reached the wall, he stopped, waited an instant, and then looked around the edge of the door casing. The room beyond the door was lighted but empty. Candles burned on the table, seven in an ornate candelabra. They flickered and danced in the breeze that came through the door. Only the lighted candles spoke of recent occupancy, and Jim went into the room.

Across from him a dark doorway told of fertile fields for further exploration, and, gripping his Colt, Jim made for it. The hall was dark throughout its length, but at the farther end a streak of light reflected on the walls. Jim moved cautiously toward the light. There were doors on either side of the hall, but for the time being he did not examine these. As he reached the end of the hall and turned toward the light, he stopped. Here was the kitchen. A big fireplace was opposite him, cranes and cooking utensils in the fireplace and on the hearth. Las Palomas' cooking arrangements were crude but plentiful. As Jim took the step that brought him beyond the door, a woman shrieked, and, turning, he saw her.

She was old, wrinkled, and toothless. So much he caught at a glance. And a glance was all that he had, for with the ending of the shriek she crouched in the corner of the room and threw her voluminous dress up over her head. From beneath the dress came a steady, but muffled, wail of fright. Jim looked across the room to where the back door, closed and barred, occupied a spot in the center of the wall, and then, assured that the kitchen was tenantless save for the woman, he turned back to the hall.

Now, as he worked along the hall, he tested the doors. Some hung open, and some were closed. At the open doors he stopped, thrust his head into the room beyond, and called softly — "Marilee? Marilee? It's Jim." — then waited for an answer. There was none.

At the closed doors, he stopped again and, testing softly, opened them. Here again he repeated his call and identification. Always his Colt was ready, always he was tense, muscles tight and waiting for any eventuality. But no response came from any of the rooms.

At the far end of the hall, almost at the lighted room, he found a closed door that did not open under his tentative pressure. Thrusting his shoulder against it, he pushed, but still the door did not give. An iron latch, heavy, hand-wrought, resisted his efforts. He rapped sharply with the muzzle of the Colt, and, face almost against the door, called: "Marilee. Marilee Clark."

Someone stirred within the room.

Jim called again, a little louder: "Marilee? Marilee!"

Now, to his listening ears, an answer came, frightened but distinct: "Who is it?"

Happiness leaped up in Jim Barre. His voice trembled with suppressed excitement as he answered. "It's Jim. Jim Barre, Marilee."

Again the door rattled under the thrust of his shoulder. Stubbornly the iron lock held. He could hear the girl striving with it.

"Stand away from the door, Marilee," he commanded. "Clear away."

Listening, he could hear movement again. Then, stepping back a short distance, he leveled the Colt. The smash of its explosion filled the hall. Twice he fired, and, lunging against the door, almost fell into the room, so suddenly did the door open.

"Marilee!" he cried.

Instantly the girl was beside him, hands on his arm, voice shaking as she spoke. "Jim! It's you! It's really you!"

"Let's get out of here," he said quickly.

"I'm ready." The girl's voice was strong when she answered. Her hands gripped his arm fiercely.

"Stay behind me," Jim ordered. "Stay close, Marilee. All right. Let's go."

Back through the doorway he went, feeling the girl's touch upon his back, so closely did she follow. Three long steps and they were in the great, lighted room where the candelabra stood. Jim Barre blinked, adjusting his eyes to the lights; then, crossing the room toward the door, he stopped short. A man came through the door, a short, heavy-set man, plump with good living, his handsome dark face crowned with a mane of black hair. For an instant, the two stood confronting each other, each halted by surprise. Then, reaching back, Jim Barre shoved Marilee, sending her reeling away. In the doorway the dark man lifted a gun and leaped swiftly to his left.

There was no word, no shout, or outcry. Jim could see the glint of light on the barrel of the gun in his opponent's hand. His own Colt was raised, and across the room the guns hammered at each other, blaring their hatred in fire and smoke and lead. Jim saw white plaster spurt from the wall beside the door, and then the dark man jerked, rising on his toes and dropping his arm woodenly to his side. Jim did not hear the gun fall. He saw the man come down from toes to heels, and slump heavily against the wall. Then, with little mewing sounds, such as a starving kitten makes, the man hitched along, squirming against the wall, his dark eyes wide and frightened, and fixed on Jim's face. Mechanically Jim lowered his weapon, flipped open the loading gate with his thumb, pulled the hammer to half cock. He did not look at his weapon as he jacked out the shells and filled the cylinder from his belt loops. He watched the man he had shot, watched him reach the corner and there slide down, leaving a dark, ugly smear on the white plaster.

"Jim." Marilee's word was a whisper.

Jim Barre turned, and with one long step reached the girl.

She was on her feet, face white, eyes big, hair disheveled, her hands held out toward him. He caught one of those extended hands and pulled her toward the door. Out of that lighted room they went, onto the porch. There, where the shadows were thick and dark, Jim paused briefly. Before them the gate to the courtyard gaped wide. As Jim looked, a man came running toward them through the gate. Jim swept up the Colt and then stayed, finger on the trigger. The running man came on, went through the door, and his voice rose shrilly: "Agapito!"

Jim's grasp tightened on the girl's hand.

"Agapito! Agapito!"

Now the man and girl moved again toward the eastern wall of the courtyard, where a small, two-wheeled, wooden *carreta* stood, its shafts resting on the hard-packed earth. Reaching the cart, Jim lifted the girl up into its bed and jumped up after her. The wooden side boards of the cart, poles with other poles across them, made a ladder. Jim went up that ladder, reached down for Marilee, and lifted. She, too, came up the poles, climbing nimbly as a cat. Jim swung her to the top of the wall, reached a long leg across, and joined her there. Then they went down, dropping into the shelter of the shadow outside the wall.

Behind them voices lifted, calling. To the west there were shouts, gunfire, and barking dogs. Just for an instant the two crouched beside the wall, and then, leading the girl with him, Jim ran for a rough pole fence, reached it, and went along its length, still toward the east.

They reached the end of the fence, ran from that shelter to the shadow of a shed, crept through its protective shade, and there, before them, dim in the moonlight, lay open country, black-spotted with brush. Marilee's hand closed convulsively on Jim's. Then they were running across the first open space, breathlessly, desperately. They ran perhaps fifty yards. Then, pulling the girl, Jim Barre rounded the first black clump of brush and dropped, panting, in its shelter. They were out of Las Palomas!

For a short time they rested there, recovering their breaths, listening to the little town seethe and stir. Thoughts flashed through Jim's mind, swift ideas, plans. Waco was west of the town, and Waco was waiting for Jim, would wait for him at the jog of the road where the big mesquite marked the trail. But Jim could not reach Waco. Alone he could have made it, but not with Marilee. Her safety came first. He must get her away. It was impossible to join Waco, to cover all that distance. Waco could wait, but, if he knew the circumstances, he would not expect Jim to come. It was up to Waco to look out for himself and, mounted, he could do it.

They were on foot, one man and one girl, and Jim must get Marilee to safety. Safety was across the river, north in Texas. He could not hope to get horses. To go back into Las Palomas and attempt to steal a horse would be foolhardy. Jim did not think of how foolhardy he had already been. That was past. Not ten minutes ago, he had only himself to look out for. Now he had Marilee.

There was just one thing to do. He must get Marilee across the river and into Texas, and he must do it as quickly as possible. Pajaritos would be the closest place, Pajaritos with its river crossing and its houses and its people. Once in Pajaritos, they would be safe. From the *pueblito* they could go on, back to the north, to Ringold's camp.

For an instant Jim Barre thought bitterly of Ringold and the rangers. If he and Waco had only waited! But there was no time for self-recrimination now. He lifted himself to his feet and drew the girl up beside him.

"We're out of there, Marilee," he whispered. "Now we'll go."

The girl was close against him, her arms around his body, her face pressed against his chest. She was sobbing, soundlessly. Awkwardly Jim lifted his hand toward her head and then, realizing that the hand still held his Colt, lowered it again.

"Don't!" he said sternly. "Don't you break down now. We've got to go." His hands were rough as he thrust the girl away.

Marilee caught her breath in one long, racking sob, and then straightened.

"Good girl," Jim praised. "Come on, now. Careful!"

From the shelter of that first brush growth to the shelter of the next, he led her, running where he must, pulling the girl along, keeping the brush always between them and Las Palomas. On they went, up the eastern slope of the valley, using shelter, looking back to where the lights of Las Palomas showed, listening to the dimming voices of the place. Now and then, in the concealment of some growth, they stopped to catch their breaths and listen. Where the brush was open, they ran, hand in hand, the man urging the girl along. And finally they reached the top of the rise and, crossing beyond it, were safe. Jim Barre took a great breath and let it go slowly.

"We're all right now," he said matter-of-factly. "Now we'll hit for the river an' home."

With the girl's hand still in his own, Jim started down the slope, northwest toward the river and Pajaritos. As they walked, a fresh fury of firing, faint in the distance, broke out from behind them. Jim winced. Was it Waco that had caused that fresh outbreak? Had the little man come into Las Palomas after his partner?

Neither Marilee nor Jim spoke as they made their way down the slope. What was there to say? What questions could be asked and answered, what explanations made? Many, surely, but this was not the time. There was a weariness upon Jim now that the first part of his objective was accomplished, a dead weight of fatigue. And as for Marilee, the girl was numb, unable to realize that she had been snatched out of her captivity, unable to believe that she was free.

At the bottom of the slope, where the hill fell away into the comparative level of the valley bottom, Marilee gave a little moan and collapsed, dropping to the ground in a little huddle. Jim, kneeling swiftly to seek the cause of this disaster, saw one small foot protruding from beneath her skirt. There was no shoe on the foot, only the ragged top of a stocking remained, and, when he touched the foot, his hand felt blood.

Pity and admiration welled up in him as he straightened. How brave this girl was, how game! Never a word of complaint, never a whimper. She had gone barefooted over that rough country, gone on and on until she could go no farther. Stooping, Jim gathered Marilee up in his arms and stared across the dimly lit country. He would have to carry her. Holding the girl high against his chest, he started forward.

And now the nightmare began. The ground was rough underfoot, and there were rocks and sand. There was grass that tried to trip the man, and there was low-growing brush. Still Jim trudged on, carrying his burden. Sometimes, perforce, he put the girl down and rested. Then, lifting her again, resting her body across his shoulder now, for he could not long carry that dead weight in his arms, he went forward. On occasion he tripped. Twice he fell. Again and again he stopped to rest. It became a dull agony of effort, of dogged persistence.

The moonlight died, and against the eastern hills the dawn came, soft and gray and rosy, and then hard as steel. Still they went on. And now small cañons beset Jim, little arroyos that were steep and treacherous. At last, he found a trail, well-traveled, that bent toward the north and east, and setting foot on the trail, Jim was dully thankful for the comparative ease it brought him. His boots were cut, rent by sharp rocks. Every step was a blunted agony. Then the trail dipped down and down, and in the growing morning light the river lay before him. Across the river were small houses and a herd of goats that lifted their heads to stare, and a boy that yelled shrilly and ran from his charges.

The river was cold and soothing to Jim's feet, and the burden on his shoulder was a leaden weight that he seemed to have carried always. The current tugged at his waist. Rocks rolled underfoot, and he staggered and almost fell. And then the water was falling away, and he was staggering up the bank, and the urchin who herded the goats was shrilling: "¡Mira, mira, Papa! ¡Ven acá!"

Up the rocky shore, Jim lurched, and then to softer footing. A house was immediately before him, then a woman's face, her dark eyes wide with excitement and query. Jim Barre stopped, and on his shoulder Marilee sagged, limp as a sack from which the contents had been drained.

"I want . . . ," Jim began dully, speaking in Spanish.

Then the weight was being lifted from him. Something was pushing him, half pushing, half lifting, and a voice from far away was murmuring: *"El pobre . . . el pobre."* After that he was being lowered down and down until the earth came up and engulfed him. Something was pressed against his lips, and he drank, swallowing water that was cool and sweet. And then his head tipped back, and all was dim and far away. So far away.

About Jim Barre, the people of Pajaritos stood looking down at him, chattering shrilly, questions and conjectures flashing back and forth. And then, above all those voices, another rose, and the woman who had first come out, who had answered the goatherd's shrill call, came pushing through to where Jim lay. She was an old woman, but vigorous, and her tongue was a lash. At her command men carried Jim into the house and stretched him on a pallet spread on the floor. Across the little room, the only room of the house, Marilee lay upon another pallet, breathing shallowly, her eyes closed, the rise and fall of her breast the only sign of life.

Jim did not see Marilee, and only dimly heard the voices. He was tired, tired, tired. He drew in one long breath, and let it go in one great sigh, and then his half-closed eyes completely closed. Jim Barre had accomplished his mission. He had finished his task. All the force that had driven him was drained away, and fatigue, pressing down upon him, he knew no more.

About him, in the room and outside the house, the scanty population of Pajaritos congregated. They had no love for a *gringo,* these people. They had been frightened. They had been beset. One of their own had been killed. They had, within hours, buried Manuel Sanchez, their fellow, and, too, they had buried others of their race, men who had been killed by the *gringos.* But they were simple people, and, while re-

sentment ran deeply, here was a man who had come out of the
south, worn and weary, carrying a woman. The ways of the
gringo were beyond their simple comprehension. They
wanted only to live and to be left alone. Moreover, beside the
gringo the white-haired woman stood, the matriarch of the vil-
lage, the one who had lived the longest and who had the
shrillest tongue. She used it now.

"Go away!" she cackled, and, moving with just such a gesture as a farm wife makes as she shoos chickens from her
doorstep, she advanced upon them.

"Go away . . . all of you!"

The men of Pajaritos, their children and their wives,
turned to obey that command, moving slowly away until only
the wide, curious eyes of the children at the door remained to
watch Jim Barre and Marilee.

Up river, fifteen miles from Pajaritos, horsemen splashed
across a ford and gained the northern bank. They paused
there, the leaders waiting until the last man cleared the
stream. They were weary men, and some of the riders wore
bandages, the cloths that bound their wounds bloodstained.
Nate Ringold, looking back toward the southern wall of the
cañon, spoke bitterly and briefly.

"An' that's all the good we did. When word gets to Austin
that we went across, I've lost my job."

Waco Ibolt, also looking at that southern bank, hardly
heard the ranger's statement. "Jim got her," he rasped. "If
we'd looked. . . ."

"We'd never have found 'em," completed Ringold. "We
did look. An' we waited where you said. Your pardner didn't
come."

Turning from the river, the tall man started up the steep
trail, his men following. One of them touched Waco's arm,

and Oscar, of his own volition, wearily fell in place. Up they went, the horses climbing slowly. On the shoulders of every man there was the weight of fatigue, and in the mind of every man was the weight of a mission that had failed. But in Waco Ibolt's mind there was a greater weight and a greater weariness. Jim was gone. Jim Barre, his partner. And it was useless to go back. Useless.

At the top of the trail Ringold stopped. "There's one more chance," he said slowly. "Just one more. We've got to go to camp, but first we'll go to Pajaritos. Maybe. . . ." He stopped. There was no use in raising a false hope. Leading the way, his horse walking, head hung low, Nate Ringold led his men. And, as they followed along the river toward the little settlement, so, too, rode other men. Leslie Tayler, concern and anxiety in his mind, rode down the creek toward the crossing of the Río Grande. Stupe Wadell, astride Jim Barre's Monte horse, his feet in the stirrups of the Mexican saddle, scanned the sprawling, deep-printed tracks of Jim Barre's feet, and he wore an evil grin as he followed them.

Eighteen

Shoot-out

How long Jim lay in a coma, utterly exhausted, he did not know. When finally he roused, he saw a wrinkled, toothless face bent above him, concern written plainly in every line. Noting his return to consciousness, the face grinned and a shrill, cackling voice asked how he felt.

Jim tried to sit up and could not. A firm, but claw-like, hand pushed him back upon his pallet, and the shrill voice demanded that he be quiet.

"The *señorita?*" Jim questioned. "Is she . . . ?"

"She is sleeping. She was very tired."

By turning his head, Jim could see that this was true. Marilee, utterly relaxed, lay not five feet away. As Jim looked, she moaned softly in her sleep, and one small hand closed convulsively. Jim struggled to a sitting position. This time there was no opposition to his movement. His female mentor was not at his side, but across the room delving into a box beside the fireplace.

She returned, carrying a jug, and put it to Jim's lips. The fiery *aguardiente* burned his mouth and throat, and hit his belly like the jolt of a blow. His eyes watered, and, lifting a hand, he wiped away the tears.

"Good, no?" The old woman smiled.

"Very good," Jim answered gratefully. *"Gracias."*

"More?" The jug was raised.

"No more," Jim said.

The wrinkled woman put the jug on the hard-packed dirt floor. Grinning, she produced corn husks and tobacco from somewhere about her person, and began the fashioning of a cigarette. Jim reached for the makings, and the woman placed them in his hand.

He rolled his cigarette and, striking a match, lit first the old woman's, then his own smoke. For a moment or two they puffed companionably. It seemed to Jim that the tension was gone, that the weight had sloughed from his shoulders. This was Pajaritos, and they were safe. His feet throbbed and burned, but the brandy in his belly warmed him and gave him strength. Removing the cigarette, he smiled and was answered by a toothless grin.

"We," he began. "The *señorita* and I. . . ." He stopped.

Voices sounded outside the little rock room in which they sat, and the old woman waggled her cigarette at Jim and, rising, hurried out the door.

Jim sat waiting, looking at Marilee. How small she was, lying there, and how sweet. Her breast rose and fell rhythmically, and one hand, flung out toward Jim, was small as a child's, or so it seemed. In Jim a protective urge welled up. Marilee. He would look after her as long as he lived. Nothing would ever touch her; nothing would ever harm her again. The old native woman came scurrying back into the room, her face anxious.

"Two men are coming. *Señor* Tayler from there" — she pointed to the north — "and the other. . . ." Her pointing hand swept to the south.

Two men! Tayler and another, coming to Pajaritos. Jim scrambled up. Fire from his torn feet shot up his legs, and he took a staggering step and would have fallen, had it not been for a quick and scrawny arm. Lowered back to the pallet, he watched the woman swing the door shut and drop a bar across it. Turning, she held a finger to her lips, commanding silence. Jim, sitting there, lifted his Colt from his holster and, holding it in his hands, faced the door.

A hoof clinked on stone. There was the scuffling sound of a horse stopping, and then Stupe Wadell's voice said: "By Satan, Tayler, I'm glad to see you. I . . . wait, man! Damn it, don't do that!"

The voice that answered was so thick with anger as to be unrecognizable, yet Jim knew that it was Tayler's. The rancher cursed Wadell, present and past back to Wadell's remotest ancestry. Finally the voice stopped for lack of breath. Into the pause Wadell threw words.

"That ain't doin' you no good, Tayler."

Apparently, however, the words had brought some measure of sanity to the man who owned the Hatchet Ranch. Tayler spoke more evenly.

"You stole the guns! You an' Fox. I went out yesterday an' found 'em gone. An' you killed Tony. I'd sent him to warn you an' Agapito. Don't try to lie out of it. I saw Tony, an' it was you who killed him."

Wadell did not answer the accusation.

After the pause, Tayler's voice went on, the triumph in it carrying to the hidden listener. "I was headed for Las Palomas to get Agapito to help me run you down. Now I'll take you across, Wadell. When we get done workin' on you, you'll be glad to tell us where you hid them guns. I'll give 'em to him an' not charge him a cent. It'll be worth it to hear you yell. Turn around and get goin'."

Again a pause.

Then Wadell said: "It's no dice, Tayler. Agapito's dead. The rangers hit Las Palomas last night, an' Agapito an' Fox both checked out. They're fightin' over there now to see who takes Agapito's place. You wouldn't last a minute in Las Palomas. I got out just in time. They're blamin' you for double-crossin' 'em here an' runnin' 'em into the rangers . . . an' they're blamin' me for bringing the Clark girl over to Las Palomas."

"That's a lie!"

"It's the truth. Barre came in ahead of the rangers an' got the girl. He killed Agapito. It ain't safe in Mexico for you, or me, neither, Tayler."

Jim almost grinned. Thieves had fallen out, and Stupe Wadell had fled to Texas for safety. He hadn't found it. Tayler was on the rampage, and Wadell was out of luck. The ranchman's next words said so.

"Then I'll fix you right now. You dirty. . . ."

"Wait, Tayler! You an' me got to stay together." Wadell's voice was desperate. "I got that saddle. I was bringin' it to you. Put down that gun. We got to talk."

Jim heard leather creak. Tayler said raspingly: "I'll talk to you, but first you unhook your belt an' drop your gun. I don't trust you, an' I've got the drop."

A pause and something thumped on the ground.

Wadell said surlily: "Now are you satisfied?"

Leather creaked again as Taylor dismounted. "Where'd you get the saddle, Stupe? How come?" He was not so wrathful now.

"In Las Palomas. Barre lost his horse, an' I found it. I pulled out to bring the saddle over to you, Tayler. Honest I did. Don't that show I'm on the square?"

"It shows that you had to get out of Las Palomas." Tayler's laugh was a harsh bark. "All right, then. I won't kill you. I'll let you go because you brought the saddle."

"That ain't all. There's somethin' else. Barre an' the girl are on this side. I found their tracks. They came across the ford. You need me, Tayler, an' I need you. You've got to find them two. If you don't, we're done."

"Barre and the girl?" Tayler's voice was thoughtful.

"The Clark girl. They're some place here. Maybe in Pajaritos. You got to get rid of them. You know that."

There was a moment's pause while Tayler thought. Then: "All right, Stupe, but where did you take the guns?"

"To the old shack by the upper crossin'. It was Fox that was to blame. He talked me into it. I didn't want to double-cross you."

"That's a lie. But if Barre an' the girl are over here. . . ."

"They're here. Look, Tayler." Wadell's voice was eager. "Once you find them an' they're out of the way, you'll be rich. We can find that mine. We can trade the guns with whoever takes Agapito's place, an' get in right with him. We can. . . ."

"I know what we can do. But if Barre ever gets to Ringold, we won't do nothin'. You think they're here in Pajaritos?"

"They've got to be. The tracks came to the ford. They were afoot. They. . . ."

"Then let's look for them."

Jim pushed himself up. The Colt hampered him, and he holstered it. Now was the time to go. Now was the time to show himself and take a hand. Marilee was in this little rock room, and, if he waited, she was in danger.

These were the men who had killed Dale Clark, who had murdered Chino Joe, who had shot Thad Gaskin. All the villainy, all the trouble, all the arson and death along the river, lay at their feet. Jim Barre did not differentiate between them, did not check the score against each. They were guilty, and he sentenced them together. And if, in executing that sentence, he himself was to be killed, still he had no choice. The hands were dealt. Torn feet forgotten, everything forgotten save that now he must play his cards, Jim took a staggering step and reached the door. His hands rested on the bar, lifting it from the sockets. Carefully he put the wooden beam on the floor, and the door swung open soundlessly on its leather hinges. Gripping the door casing for support, Jim looked out.

Neither Tayler nor Wadell saw the movement of the door. They were in front of the house, twenty feet away, facing each other, and Wadell's gun and belt lay at his feet. Monte stood behind Wadell, the battered saddle on his back, his buckskin head hung low.

Tayler's voice was harsh with strain. "Here?"

"Right here," Wadell agreed. "Some place in Pajaritos. They couldn't have gone farther. We'll look an'. . . ."

"No need of lookin', Stupe," Jim said quietly.

As one, the men turned. For an instant blank surprise was fully upon their faces. Behind Jim, Marilee's voice arose, calling his name.

"Jim! Jim!"

Jim took a lurching step away from the door, the rough rock of the wall grating against his shoulders. Tayler's gun was in his hand, and now, recovering from his surprise, he jerked it up and fired one hasty shot. Rock dust and chips flew from the wall beside Jim's head. Monte was running, and Tayler's horse had whirled around, away from the frightening explosion. Smooth walnut filled Jim's grasp. Steel slid from leather. Deliberately his gun came up, and above its sights he saw Tayler's body. The walnut kicked sharply in his hand, once, and then again. Powder smoke, sharp and acrid, stung Jim's nostrils.

Wadell was stooping, groping wildly for the gun and belt at his feet. Tayler took one small, mincing step, then a great stride as though striving to recover his balance. He threw one arm wide, as a horseman will when his horse cuts sharply back after turning a cow, and then, spinning on his heel, he half turned and pitched forward on his face.

Lead bit Jim Barre, thrusting him back against the wall. As through a haze, he saw Wadell, crouched there before him,

187

one knee touching the ground. Wadell's hand was lifted and the muzzle of his gun was a round black hole above which the killer's squinting eyes showed. Then eyes and muzzle were hidden by a ring of flame, and again rock spurted beside Jim's head.

It seemed to Jim that his gun would never rise. It came up slowly so that the sights fell into line. Again the recoil drove into the fork of his hand, and the gun bounced up and then lowered once more, bounced again, and dropped, bounced and dropped — clicked empty.

Out there in Pajaritos' dusty street, Stupe Wadell crouched on one knee. His left hand was thrust down to support himself, and his right hand half raised. Seemingly, Wadell was surprised that he could not complete the lifting of that hand. His eyes were wide with blank astonishment as he tried. Then, sudden as an axe stroke, the supporting arm gave way, and Wadell pitched over on his side, and, turning, lay upon his back.

Slowly, legs widespread like a drunken man, Jim came forward from the wall. He did not feel the hot blood that trickled from the wound in his side. He did not feel the protests of his tortured feet. He must be sure of this — very sure. He stopped and looked down, his empty gun dangling limply. Wadell's eyes were open, and surprise still showed in them. The man's lips moved as though he would speak. Then the light of living drained from the glaring eyes, and they were glassy and sightless as they stared up at the sky. Mechanically Jim holstered his gun and, turning, took a step back toward the rock house. And now, for the first time, he heard Marilee's voice, weak, crying out his name. "Jim!"

On his torn, battered feet, the false strength draining out of him, Jim staggered forward. He did not see the dark and curious faces at the doors of the houses on either side. He did

not see a man come furtively out and then, suddenly embold-
ened, walk to Wadell's body. He saw nothing but that empty
door. He reached it, catching the casing to steady himself.
Marilee was sitting up, her face turned toward him, eyes wide
with fright and hair disheveled. The old woman knelt by
Marilee, supporting her, and, as Jim paused, the girl tried
vainly to rise.

Two more lurching steps Jim took, and then dropped
down beside Marilee. Her arms were tight about his neck,
holding him, and her tears were wet upon his cheek. Jim's
own arms closed about her.

How long he knelt there he did not know or care. Marilee
was in his arms, held close. Then, suddenly, he was aware of
movement. The native woman was on her feet, bent forward
intently, listening. Her voice was sharp when she spoke.

"More horsemen are coming!"

It was true. Jim could hear them now, horses coming at a
run over the rocky ground. He freed his arms and would have
risen, but Marilee held him, her face against his chest as she
sobbed.

The horses thundered to a stop outside, and dust swirled
up in Pajaritos' street. There were exclamations and curses,
and then the door was darkened. Little Waco Ibolt stood
there, his hand resting on his gun, surprise ludicrous upon his
weathered face. Behind Waco was Ringold, and behind the
captain other faces showed.

"Jim!" Amazement was in Waco's voice, and thankful-
ness, a pæan of gratitude to the lords of chance. "Jim! My
gentle Nellie!"

Waco came striding forward, Ringold's hand upon his
shoulder, shoving him along. Then the small room was filled
with men and voices, and Jim, holding Marilee against his
side, felt the last strength drain out of him and was aware,

once more, of weariness and pain.

"Tayler," he said needlessly and dully, "an' Stupe Wadell. Waco, I. . . ."

Strong hands seized him and moved him carefully, easing him down. He could see Ringold's stern face, the corner of his grizzled mustache caught between his lips.

"We saw 'em, Jim," the ranger captain said. "Just take it easy. It's all done now."

Nineteen

Peace on the Border

Waco Ibolt, seated on the edge of the board sidewalk in front of Bill Murry's small white house in Carver City, produced his stockman's knife from his pocket and split a generous portion from the edge of a plank. Murry, rotund and cheerful, sat beside the little man, staring at him.

There had been much activity for Bill Murry since the arrival of the morning mail, and now, with dinner over, he was taking his ease and getting a little information. In a general way Murry knew what had happened at Pajaritos, at Las Palomas, and the Hatchet Ranch, but he wanted the whole story.

"So," he said, "Tayler talked to you an' Ringold?"

"Yeah," Waco agreed. "He talked. He was layin' there with two Forty-Five slugs in his belly, an' he knew he was goin' to die. He told us all about it."

"An' all the grief was over that old saddle," Murry mused.

"Every bit of it." Waco whittled at his pine splinter. "Tayler had made a deal with Howie Clark. Howie had bought Tayler's interest in the Hatchet, an', when Howie was killed, Tayler couldn't find the sales contract. He thought it was in the saddle, an' sure enough it was. An' he had an idea that Howie had drawed a map of the mine he'd found. An' that was right, too. Neither of them things was found on Howie, an', when Chino Joe kept sayin' the saddle was valuable an' that he had promised to get it to Dale an' Marilee, Tayler had a hunch that what he wanted was in the saddle."

"Jim's given that bill of sale to a lawyer," Murry said. "It

191

looks like Marilee will get the Hatchet, her bein' the only heir."

"Looks like it!" Waco exclaimed. "The lawyer *said* she'd get it."

"What else did Tayler tell you?" Murry urged.

"The whole damned thing," Waco answered. "Jim had it doped out. He figured it all out from the things he'd seen an' heard, I'll tell you." Waco whittled at the splinter again, collected his thoughts, and then continued.

In substance, his tale was the same as that Jim Barre had told him while they waited for the moon to rise before crossing the Río Grande. There were few differences, few points of variation. Leslie Tayler, dying, cleansing his mind before he died, had been lucid and very complete in his confession. Waco spoke of Dale Clark's death, of how the two Lemoine brothers, already working for Tayler in his gunrunning enterprise and crazy to discover Howie Clark's lost mine, had brought Stupe Wadell into the picture. He spoke of how Chino Joe had been killed and his body dumped into the Río Grande. He told of how Tayler's cupidity, his reaching out for more money, had brought about his downfall.

"If Tayler had been satisfied just to steal the Hatchet from the Clark kids and not mix up in this gun-runnin' an' minehuntin' business, he'd be alive today," Waco declared. "But he wasn't. He spread himself too thin."

Murry nodded. He could understand that statement.

"An' if he hadn't rung in Stupe Wadell, he might have been all right," Waco continued. "You see, Stupe was crazy. He would hit a man, an' then he couldn't stop. It was Stupe that beat Dale an' Chino Joe to death. An' he killed Tayler's cook the same way, Tayler said."

There was silence for a moment after Waco's statement, and then the little man spoke again. "It was me that done the

192

real smart thing," he said with boyish pride. "When I sold Tayler Jim's good saddle in place of givin' him that old Mexican hull. That was what was smart. Jim might've figured it out, but where would he've been if I hadn't done that job for him?"

Murry, suppressing a grin, looked from the corners of his eyes at the speaker. "Yeah," he agreed, "that was smart."

Waco closed his knife with a snap and returned it to his pocket.

"But you'd all have been in the soup if Ringold hadn't come over into Mexico," Murry said.

"Ringold would have been in the soup if he hadn't," retorted Waco. "He'd have had the whole state of Texas down on him if he'd left a kidnapped Texas girl over there. The way it is, he's a hero. An' he was worryin' about losin' his job, too!" The little man's snort was contemptuous. "Shucks, if they tried to fire Ringold right now, us Texans would just rise up an' throw the governor out of office. That's what we'd do."

"Anyhow," Murry stated, "he done it. That's the main thing. An' with Agapito de Griego killed, Ringold ain't likely to have any more trouble down there soon."

"He ain't goin' to have none anyhow," Waco announced. "I'm due to go back to the Hatchet an' look after it for Marilee. There's some kind of a legal jackpot that's got to be settled first, but I'm the fellow that's goin' down there."

Again Bill Murry looked from the corners of his eyes and smiled slyly. "Think Jim will keep you on?" he drawled.

"Jim?" Waco demanded, turning to stare at Murry. "Oh . . . yeah, I *sabe*. You mean that Jim an' Marilee are goin' to get hitched. Yeah. I reckon they will. I ain't worried none about Jim an' me. Not a bit. Marilee, neither."

"When do you think it'll come off?" questioned Murry.

"Jim and Marilee, I mean."

"The weddin'?" Waco asked. "I dunno. Marilee's feet are all tore to rags. It'll take them a while to heal, an' Jim is kind of a cripple himself, hobblin' around in carpet slippers. An' then Marilee's broke up pretty bad about Thad Gaskin bein' killed. She's had a bad shock, bein' kidnapped an' all, an' then havin' Jim snake her out of there like he did. It's goin' to take a while. I'd say they'd get married this spring, though. I'd bet on that."

Waco picked his teeth with the clean sliver left from his whittling. "Your wife's a whale of a good cook, Bill," he confided. "It's mighty nice of her to have Jim an' Marilee here an' to look after 'em."

"Jane likes the girl," Murry said. "Well. . . ." He stood up. "It's about time for me to go downtown. Got to get to work."

Waco also arose. "An' I got a few things to do, too. Before you go, Bill, I got a proposition to put up to you."

Bill Murry paused.

"Now listen." Waco said earnestly.

From the window of the marshal's house, Jim Barre could look out on the street. He saw Waco and Murry, sitting side by side on the edge of the walk. Jim's feet were encased in voluminous carpet slippers, and they hurt, but, watching Waco, Jim forgot the ache. Waco, good little man. Waco, good partner. And Bill Murry, solid and stolid, and a man that you could count on. And Mrs. Murry, how good she was.

Who but Bill Murry would have taken in a homeless girl and a man who had no more than a horse, a bed, and an old saddle? Who but Jane Murry would have mothered and cared for them? Jim Barre didn't know. And Waco! How he had taken hold. Waco had run things. To be sure, Nate Ringold had helped, and deserved credit, but Ringold had his duty to follow and to hold him. Ringold was already on his way back to the camp at the Hatchet Ranch above Pajaritos.

It had been Ringold and Waco who, in a spring wagon taken from the Hatchet, had hauled Jim Barre and Marilee to Saunders and put them on the train. Ringold was keeping an eye on the Hatchet now. He had seen to the burial of Thad Gaskin, had taken charge of the bodies of Stupe Wadell and Leslie Tayler. Nate Ringold had made things easy for Jim Barre and for Marilee. Nate Ringold was all right.

But where would a man find a partner like Waco? Nowhere. When Waco was made, the mold was broken. Little, irascible, crotchety Waco! He had run errands for Jim Barre, he had brought the doctor and the lawyer, the attorney who would handle Marilee's affairs and who, in time, would restore the Hatchet Ranch to her, its rightful owner. Waco had been cheerful; he had gone through; he was always with a man, and you never had to look back to find him. Jim Barre had ridden the river with Waco. He knew the little man's worth. He smiled gently as he looked at Waco's small straight back. The smile broadened as he saw Waco, looking up at Bill Murry, gesticulate.

"Marilee's asking for you, Jim," Jane Murry said softly from the doorway.

Jim got up. Shuffling in the carpet slippers that covered his swollen feet, he made his way to the bedroom. At the door he stopped.

Marilee lay on the bed, her hair a thick brown braid upon the whiteness of the pillow. Her face, thin with strain, was turned toward the door and her eyes, big and dark, fixed on Jim Barre.

There she was, safe, cared for. Jim placed his hand upon the door casing and watched her. What had he, Jim Barre, to offer a girl like that? He was broke. His horse, his saddle, his bed comprised his sole wealth. What had he to offer?

"Jim."

Releasing his hold upon the casement, Jim crossed the room toward the bed. Marilee's thin hand made a little gesture, and he sat down gingerly on Mrs. Murry's clean coverlet.

"Yes?" he said tentatively.

"I just wanted to make sure that you were here." The girl's voice trembled a trifle. "I wanted to be sure, Jim."

"I'm here, Marilee," Jim assured her.

"You won't leave me?"

"I'll not leave you."

"You'll never leave me, Jim? Never, never?" The thin hand stole out and touched Jim's. For a moment they were still very quiet, then Jim Barre's big arm slipped under Marilee's shoulders, lifting her until, with a contented sigh, she rested against his chest.

"Never, Jim?" Voice and eyes were child-like, trusting, questing.

"Never," he said hoarsely. "Never, Marilee."

The lips that met his own were not those of a child, but a woman.

Out on the sidewalk, Waco finished his proposition. "There it is," he said. "That's the way of it, Bill. Of course, we'll take Jim an' Marilee an' Ringold in with us."

Bill Murry nodded.

"An' now," Waco said, "I'll walk downtown with you. I got to get my saddle an' stuff an' have it sent up to your house, an' I've got to get Jim's bed an' that Mexican saddle, too. Jim sets a store by that saddle. You want to go by the dépôt while I get 'em?"

"I'll go with you," agreed Murry. "I've got nothin' pressin'."

"It'll be just open an' shut." Waco made a gesture to show how simple the whole thing was. "I'll keep my eyes open. I already know that country across the river pretty well, an', huntin' strays an' such, I'll be bound to know it better. That map of Clark's was all rubbed out by the silver on the saddle horn. It ain't worth a hoot, but that don't matter. Time I've been down there a while, I'll draw a map myse'f an' then you an' me an' the rest'll be rich. There ain't no mine that can stay lost. None of 'em. An' when we locate the one that Howie Clark found. . . ."

Waco's boots thumped on the sidewalk as he walked beside Bill Murry, and in the eyes of both there was a light — the vision of Golconda.

ALAN LeMAY

SPANISH CROSSING

The stories in this classic collection, in paperback for the first time, include "The Wolf Hunter," a gripping tale of a loner who makes his living hunting wolves for bounty and the crafty coyote who torments him. Old Man Coffee, one of LeMay's most memorable characters, finds himself in the midst of a murder mystery in "The Biscuit Shooter." In "Delayed Action," Old Man Coffee's challenge is to vindicate a lawman who's been falsely accused. These and many other fine stories display the talent and skill of one of the West's greatest storytellers.